His message focused on t[...] attitude of the people. He [...] issues of life and that no external force, however great and overwhelming, can at long destroy a people if it does not first win the victory of the spirit against them. Jesus was the product of the constant working of the creative mind of God upon the life, thought, and the character of humanity.

-Howard Thurman, *Jesus and the Disinherited*, page 21, ff.

"I tell you if I had a white man who understood Negroes, I'd have to let Mr. Guizac go, she said and stood up again. The priest turned then and looked her in the face. "He has nowhere to go. Dear lady, I know you well enough to know you wouldn't turn him out for a trifle" and without waiting for an answer he raised his hand and gave her his blessing in a rumbling voice. She smiled angrily and said, "I didn't create his situation of course."

The priest let his eyes wander to the birds. They had reached the middle of the lawn. The cock stopped suddenly and curving his neck backwards he raised his tail and spread it with a shimmering timbrous noise. Tiers of small pregnant suns floated in a green-gold haze over his head. The priest stood transfixed his jaw slack. Mrs. MacIntyre wondered where she had ever seen such an idiotic old man. "Christ will come like that!" He said in a loud, gay voice, and wiped his hand over his mouth and stood there gazing.

Mrs. MacIntyre's face assumed a set puritanical expression and she reddened. Christ in the conversation embarrassed her the way sex had her mother. "It is not my responsibility that Mr. Guizac has nowhere to go," she said. "I do not find myself responsible for all of the extra people in the world." The old man didn't seem to hear her. His attention was fixed on the cock who was taking minute steps backward, his head against the spread tail. "The Transfiguration" he murmured.

She had no idea what he was talking about. "Mr. Guizac didn't have to come here in the first place," she said giving him a hard look. The cock lowered his tail and began to pick grass. "He didn't have to come in the first place," she repeated, emphasizing each word. The old man smiled absently. "He came to redeem us," he said and blandly reached for her hand and shook it and said he must go."

--Flannery O'Connor, *The Displaced Person*

Pittsburgh Jesus

A. Christian van Gorder and Dred Scott

Copyright © 2011 A. Christian van Gorder and Dred Scott

All rights reserved. No part of this book may be used or reproduced by any means, graphic, electronic, or mechanical, including photocopying, recording, taping or by any information storage retrieval system without the written permission of the publisher except in the case of brief quotations embodied in critical articles and reviews.

WestBow Press books may be ordered through booksellers or by contacting:

WestBow Press
A Division of Thomas Nelson
1663 Liberty Drive
Bloomington, IN 47403
www.westbowpress.com
1-(866) 928-1240

Because of the dynamic nature of the Internet, any Web addresses or links contained in this book may have changed since publication and may no longer be valid. The views expressed in this work are solely those of the author and do not necessarily reflect the views of the publisher, and the publisher hereby disclaims any responsibility for them.

Any people depicted in stock imagery provided by Thinkstock are models, and such images are being used for illustrative purposes only.

Certain stock imagery © Thinkstock.

ISBN: 978-1-4497-0783-5 (sc)
ISBN: 978-1-4497-0784-2 (dj)
ISBN: 978-1-4497-0782-8 (e)

Library of Congress Control Number: 2010940420

Printed in the United States of America

WestBow Press rev. date: 06/20/2011

Contents

Dedication and Acknowledgments vii

Introduction. ix

Chapter One: The Sushi Bar. 1

Chapter Two: Nativity: Pittsburgh, 1979 7

Chapter Three: Childhood 35

Chapter Four: Miracles. 69

Chapter Five: Teachings 99

Chapter Six: Parables 113

Chapter Seven: Human Encounters 121

Chapter Eight: The City. 131

Chapter Nine: The Passion 137

Chapter Ten: Resurrection and Ascension. 149

Postscript: Two Friends. 157

Dedication and Acknowledgments

Writing is always a collaborative effort. Dr. Scott would like to thank the members of the Turner Station United Methodist Church in Dundalk Maryland, for their assistance. Special thanks to the song and melody of my friend's life, Catherine Marshall Scott who has stood by the good Doctor through so many years. Dr. Scott's adopted grandmother was Mrs. Minnie Davis and his mother is Mrs. Inez Annette Heath. I would like to thank my colleague Dr. Ralph Wood and also, Jim Keener, Artyom Tonoyan, Barry Harvey, Brian Small, and Linh Tran of Baylor University for their assistance in the editing and the revising of this book.

My greatest resource in this writing springs from two distinct sources. I want to thank my many students from my years at Messiah College and Baylor University. I'd like to especially thank Derek Lehman, Femi Akkinabe, Zack Stock, John Maher, Brian Scott, Jesse Melton, Renee Leverette, Sheena Styles-King, Shanet Foust, Josanna Snyder, Grace Trabulsi, Jason Yakelis, Josiah Ludwick, Jeremiah Schofield, Mac Carr, Britney Mussler-Carr, Tonya Trask-Scott, Miostis Pineda, and Teofilo Marcelino who wrote responses on *Jesus and the Disinherited* for a course I taught at Messiah entitled *Jesus and the Black Experience*. I saved their papers and re-read these for inspiration as we began to write.

This book is lovingly dedicated to my wife, my daughters, my sister, my mother, and my grandmother. It's all about the women and always has been, and forever will be, all about the women. I grew up under the care of my German-speaking grandmother, Maria Bach Lutsch and her amazing daughter, Erika Helena Lutsch van Gorder. Life changed forever when I met my bride, Vivian Ndudi Ezeife. These eternal women have patiently nurtured me and made me who I am today. When the world outside is cold, they have filled our hearts with light. They are the suns of my universe as I was the son and the husband to their truest commitments. I fully understand why Jesus the Palestinian chose to learn so much and find solace so often in the arms of his mother Mary and in other loving women such as Mary Magdalene and Martha the wife of his friend Lazarus. It is to the women of my life that I dedicate this book.

Women, *by Alice Walker*
(From *Good Night Willie Lee, I'll See you In the Morning*, 1979)

They were women then- My mamma's generation
Husky of voice – stout of step -With fists as well as hands
How they battered down doors and ironed starched white shirts.
How they led armies, head-ragged generals across
mined fields and booby-trapped ditches-
To discover books, desks and a place for us.
How they knew what we must know without knowing a page of it themselves

Introduction

Paul writes in the book of Philippians that there is one name that is "above every other name; the name of Jesus." That name is more than a historical reference. Each of us as Christians brings countless sources of inspiration to the way we think about Jesus. For me, these have become cemented throughout a lifetime of reading newspapers, reflecting, listening, and learning within the Christian tradition. Jesus is the center and the ends on either side. The reason I wrote this book is because I have found that writing is one way to express my own love for God as shown in Jesus. The actual structure for this book comes from Luigi Santucci's timeless classic of devotional spirituality, *Meeting Jesus* (Herder and Herder, 1971). The foundational idea for this book, what would the life of Jesus have been like had he lived as an African American in our modern context, comes from Howard Thurman's *Jesus and the Disinherited* (Harper and Row, 1956).

The Italian Catholic writer Signor Luigi Santucci was born in Milan in 1918 and spent most of his life in writing and teaching. He loved the book *The Little Flowers* of St. Francis of Assisi. Santucci never apologized for the rootedness in faith of his own perspective and begins his biography of Jesus by quoting Dostoyevsky who said that if he had to choose between Christ and the truth he would chose Christ. Santucci's writing is reminiscent of the brilliant novels of the Greek Orthodox writer Nikos Kazantzakis where he wrote that faith is only real when alive in the daily experiences of life and put into practice in the context of shared relationships. Santucci said that he "had the impression of being a last-ditcher guarding a bridge for a defeated army that has long been in retreat" (page 16). For both Santucci and Kazantzakis, Christ is many things, among which is that He is a poet - the Incarnate Word - that challenges all and brings followers to a life of deep and usually inconclusive struggles, but also to a path of hope. Santucci was interested in moving the message of Christ from stale pages and familiar facades. He explained this mission in his writing when he explained:

> *"I will tell the story of Christ miracles in terms of things that are happening to us, because as soon as we think of our own lives we are all at Jericho, Bethesda, Gadara, and Lake Tiberius or in the tomb at Bethany. We've experienced blindness, paralysis, insanity, storms, and death. A thousand times we've been told "Ephrata!" and our tongues have been loosened. We've been cleansed and our sores have disappeared. We have heard him say "Come out!" and the stone of seplechures has opened to release us from our darkness"* (page 56).

The unchanging message of Jesus is like air and water and is always adapting and adjusting to the specific situations of our constantly changing lives.

Howard Thurman was an African-American Baptist who was born in 1900 in the American South and was raised by a maternal grandmother who had been a slave. Dr. Thurman grew up in a world where oppressive *Jim Crow* racism was a pressing everyday reality. Leaning on the Lord was not just a song to be sung, but was a critical way of dealing with the world. Thurman went on to study in the halls of the Euro-American academy before working at Howard University's Rankin Chapel and then founding the *Church for the Fellowship of All People* in San Francisco. Later, Dr. Thurman would travel to India with his wife Sue Bailey Thurman to learn from Mahatma Gandhi. This great theologian, teacher and writer is most famous for being Dr. King's mentor. Dr. Thurman left us in the Spring of 1981 to claim his eternal reward. In his book, *Jesus and the Disinherited*, Dr. Howard Thurman was simply trying to put into practice at the local level what he believed was truth – that the religion of Jesus was one for all of America's wall-bruised people.

In his theological reflections Dr. Thurman made a distinction between what he called the *religion of Jesus* from the *religion about Jesus.* The religion about Jesus, according to Dr. Thurman, focusing on three days and mostly six hours of the Son of Man's thirty-three year life, because such a narrow focus made the Christ of God more containable and controllable to those who wanted to be called "Christian" without the full weight of being obligated to the challenging ethical message and mandates of Jesus. This new reduced religion is one that can more easily become appropriated by people in power, comfort, wealth, and privilege and thus, could become a religion that was respectable and inoffensive. In contrast, Dr. Thurman believed that the religion of Jesus was a dynamic and challenging religion for oppressed people who often found themselves "up against a wall." This path of discipleship was not simply a feel-good religion, a cultural club, or a social group. It was a pathway of service and zeal for the truth which often led to inevitable confrontations with much of a social order rooted in systemic oppression and injustice. In the *Jim Crow* America where Dr. Thurman lived, he noticed that much of what was called the "church" was nothing more than social organizations that served as an extension of the dominant culture. In Thurman's caustic and challenging words, "The men who bought the slaves were Christians. Christian ministers quoting the Apostle Paul gave the sanction of religion to the system of slavery" (page 14).

Thurman felt that many churches had lost their "first love" for God and had become the builders and the maintainers of the walls desired by the King Herod's or the slave-owning General George Washington's of the world. When this happened, what was called the church became indistinguishable from the dominant forces of the culture. A clear message was inevitably erased by the dark forces of many within the dominant culture who had no tolerance for being confronted or opposed on ethical grounds. What emerged in *Jim Crow* America, as well as in the politico-religious world of Emperor Constantine, was that a form of Christendom came to power which seemed to be largely independent of any radical or prophetic message. For Dr. Thurman, the first and truest message of Jesus, however, was one given against the wall and was a message for those who were forgotten by the wealthy and the powerful. Thurman wrote that Jesus treated people as brothers and sisters who were beloved and created by God and not as those who should be seen to be threats or racial, social, or economic categories or simply as merely passive actors in a world created for others by others. Jesus as described by Dr. Thurman was a poor, oppressed Jew of a minority community under the domination of an oppressive status-quo. The message of Jesus was rooted in a specific place and it is this rootedness which must never be forgotten. Christ dealt with those in power, and those in control, and helped those who were asking the question in his day: "What must our attitude be toward Rome?" (Page 22).

Jesus, for Dr. Thurman, gave common people vital strategies to cope with the pain of their daily lives. Christ was a resister against evil and for what he called the Kingdom of God. The Son of Man sought to fortify His followers with an inner strength which He explained was the key to freedom. His spirit, resurrected from the dead in physical form, gave people courage to fight the oppression that they faced in their own lives. Jesus, with no economic, political, physical, or social security to speak of, fought against insecurity and fought for those who felt insecure. The man God sent to the earth to walk among us turned humiliation into humility, suffering into teaching, and crucifixion into triumph in the same way that He turned water into wine. The Christ of God taught that security had to occur between your two ears and that a person of the spirit could feel secure even though they were not at all secure politically, socially, or economically. When you give people the Kingdom of God they don't need anything else.

This book, born from these starting points, seeks to present one distinct portrait of a life lived by one who was weak who fought against the powerful. It is not the story of the Jesus of the Gospels because both Dr. Scott and I affirm that Christ was a once-and-for-all-time distinct revelation of God within humanity. Rather, it is a book about a person who was animated by some of the very same passions and visions that we've come to recognize within our own lives as being central to the message and heart of Jesus Christ. It is sad to say, but the spirit of plantation, controlling Christianity that was described by Dr. Thurman is as alive today as ever in our modern world. Our world is filled with those who deny ideas such as the physical resurrection of Christ from the dead or the plausibility of miracles and supernatural events as being purely fabrications of weak minds. We still stand as people of faith. Even though there are still some who insist that the world is flat – and free of anything that is mysterious and demand that we recant any notion of faith, Christians still whisper with Galileo of God's Holy Spirit: "…and yet it moves." Each of us will have to find our own ways to make flesh in our own places what we believe a life of truth, beauty, and love should be like. Our lives are the stories that each of us is writing and this book is our gift to you and comes in the hope that, somehow and in some way it will bring honor to the Jesus of God. Bless your bones!

Chapter One:

The Sushi Bar

Fifth and Division, 2009

Jesus Dred Scott was my friend. I don't know how else to start this book. It'd take me two lifetimes to write everything I'm thinking about.

My name is Caesar Chavez Garnica and I met Jesus in D.C. so I always think of him as a D.C. brother even though I know he wasn't born there. Jesus was born in the Steel City – Pittsburgh. The longer he's away from us, the more folks praise him like he was "all that and a bag of chips." But don't get confused and start building churches to the Pittsburgh Jesus. There are already enough churches in every crumbling, tear-filled city. The last thing we need is another panhandling God to come and take tithes from our poor, hope-filled, toothless, smiling grandmothers. Another "last thing we need" is a legion of fat old preachers counseling sweet-sounding lies into the ears of our frustrated, beautiful, girlfriends.

Two thousand years ago the Lord and Savior of the Universe Jesus Christ revealed Himself as the son of God Almighty and the perfect moment in history. However, two thousand years, is a long time ago, and the last time I checked, Jerusalem aint anywhere near Pittsburgh or D.C., or the streets of Baltimore. Did the heaven- Jesus of the gold-edged pages of the Holy Bible ever listen to Tupac or dance to Trina, or the Georgia Peach - Rasheeda, or to Lil Kim? The only Jesus that I ever met personally was Jesus Scott and he was no flying alien miracle-man passing out wise words, cream-filled chocolates, and golden roses that smelled like saffron.

Pittsburgh Jesus was much more amazing than that: he was a brother who lived out what he believed. He was magic.

Whenever I feel like I'm at the end of my rope, it is the questions that I ask that keep me going. I've experienced a lot of things in my life but I've never been bored – even for a minute. The questions I turn over in my mind are like the spice in food or the sweet slice of lemon in a tall, cold glass of much needed sweet iced tea. When I've been knocked flat off my feet, an army of questions gives me a second wind and helps me to get up. To my mind, questions are much more interesting than answers or assertions.

Some people like to know how a movie ends before they start to watch it. Maybe that's why fortune-tellers can make a living telling sweet lies to folks they'll never see again in a million years. But I'm not looking for anything as grand as answers. The questions I wrestle with somehow seem more important than any answers I may end up finding along the way. Sometimes, an answer is a let-down like the feeling you get after you open a birthday present only to find out that it's something somebody else no longer wanted and something you can't use. Life has a way of moving us around; up and down, inside and out. For me, questions make more sense than answers. My grandma used to say: a person who never questions, never learns. Isn't that the truth?

While some folks call you by your name or your nickname or feel comfortable enough to call you "brother" or nervous enough to call you "sir" or just plain "mister" – Jesus greeted everyone with a strong "Hey friend!" That may seem insignificant, but it is how I always picture Jesus. He gave everyone a chance to befriend him. I think it was his way of making folks feel invaluable. Pittsburgh used to say that his friends were his bridge. And, in my own life, all I can say is thank God for the friends that I've known along the way. If it weren't for them, life might feel like I was trying to get somewhere in a hurry without a map. Friends keep me on track and bring a song into the middle of life whenever it holds me hostage by surprise. Friends have taken me through all kinds of cloudy storms on their flying wings.

Being a friend with Pittsburgh was easier than eating a bowl of ripe cherries and harder than sanding down an old piece of wood. Sometimes he was hard to figure out or explain, but his friendship was all that really mattered.

Life is sometimes a steep road with strong winds that smash us in the face like a thrown brick. Sometimes things are so unfair and we are dealt a bad hand. My dad always reminded me that the world was unfair. Folks are being played, tricked, hustled, and abused on every street corner. Some folks are like zombies because they've been smashed down so many times that it is harder and harder for them to get back up on their feet. Some folks are like the old Muhammad Ali after all of those years of having his head being smashed week-in and week-out.

Do-gooding social workers and priests have often talked to me about injustice, but too often, these same folks make excuses when it is time for them to step up to the plate and do something personal. In the streets, justice always trickles out in spoonfuls while injustice swamps us away like Hurricane Katrina. Power gets stronger when justice gets weaker. Maybe that is what some folks mean when they say that justice is blind.

I used to try and get a front-row seat whenever some Catholic Worker or Rastafarian came up to talk to Jesus about injustice. Later, I'd argue with him about how the evils in the world were all part of a system that worked like clockwork in grinding us down if we tried to resist or to find some measure of freedom. But Pittsburgh said that all of the problems in the city would unravel once folks got their own heads on straight and took back the power the system had tried to steal from them. We disagreed about the vampires on every street, but we both knew they were hiding in check cashing stores and in every bar and strip club. Maybe PJ was right: the unraveling of injustice needed to come through some inner revolution, but I didn't think anything was gonna change very quickly with lofty dreams like that.

Talking about injustice can get depressing because problems seem like the Himalayan Mountains that haven't budged since the beginning of time. For me, poverty was always issue number one. The poor and the rich needed to change places for their own good. You never had to look for poverty because it would always find you and come and punch your teeth out. Poverty makes free folks into slaves. Cripples think that it is their fault that they are walking with a limp. At the same time, yuppie movers and the shakers seem about as poor as can be when it came to having some kindness for the poor. Pittsburgh was poor as dirt, but he never let one ounce of poverty seep into his way of looking at things. He surfed on the wave instead of falling down and drowning underneath it.

Jesus Dred Scott was never merely *for* the poor or *among* the poor; he was the poor. He was so poor he couldn't even afford to make promises. The man lived outside on the inside – he was homeless and poor. He never looked at us from the outside. He was all bruised up from beginning to end and was constantly rubbing against those sharp, ragged cutting surfaces of the wall all around us called America. He was a man of the inward center and he gave us his soul. He hated the hounds of hell: fear, hypocrisy, and hatred. Jesus Scott wanted to make folks freer- not smarter or richer, but freer.

Pittsburgh wasn't into accepting anything at face value from somebody waving a clipboard or shouting with an angry voice. He told us to make our own way and not to listen to the haters and self-righteous rule-makers. Isn't it true that every rule has an exception so who are these folks telling us what to think? Most social workers and priests ministered in the streets during the day. But at night they escape into cozy suburban homes with cable and a two-car garage. They game in two worlds and never let the two touch each other. The rest of the folks who tell you how to run their lives don't know how to run their own and don't really care about your problems. They have their own messed-up kids and marriages sicker than a crocodile with AIDS to worry about. Why give these clowns the time of day?

Most folks who want to fight you aren't worth the effort. When two dogs are scrapping over an old rag the way to stop the battle is simple: have one of the dogs let go of their end of the rag. The rags of flags, billboards, and promises in bars may make you feel good for a second, but they'll also make you wake up the next day with a headache or AIDS or something even worse. Myths make us happen. All my life I've dealt with other folk's myths – Santa Claus, Uncle Sam, and Uncle Tom – but never my own. Then, life started happening, and I met some amazing folks and saw some amazing things. I've got my own stories to tell now – I guess that means I'm getting old. I can't usually tell the difference between what is real and magical after things happen, but I'm okay with that.

Here I am working on my laptop sitting in this sushi bar on Fifth and Division in Philly. Ever since grandma bought me this computer, I've wanted to do something special - like write a book. Pittsburgh gives me some place to start. I really wish you could've known him yourself. Some of the things I'll write about will be too wild to believe. But, I saw what I saw with my own eyes. Anyway, what I have to say is still more believable than the Easter Bunny or what some politician has to say about how all of our problems will be solved if he gets elected. So, read on.

    I didn't meet Pittsburgh 'til about three years ago or so. The rest of his life comes from a lot of stories that his mother, Mama Shenice Richardson Scott, and others have told me. Even if some of the stories aren't true they are good enough and they should be true....

Chapter Two:
Nativity: Pittsburgh, 1979

1. Jesus of the Streets

Jesus Scott was born in Pittsburgh, Pennsylvania. That is how he came to be nicknamed "Pittsburgh." He grew up in the streets of Harrisburg, so the people from there will probably end up calling him the Jesus of Harrisburg. Since he was killed in D.C. – and that's where I knew him – you could've called him "D.C. Jesus." He also traveled the streets of Philly, New York, and Bal-mer so; you could also call him "New York," "Baltimore," or the "Philadelphia Jesus."

After he was born, I'm not sure if Jesus Scott ever went back to Pittsburgh, but, who knows, maybe he is there right now. He always talked about his tough Steelers and how he grew up surrounded by green hills and valleys. I guess that he was only a little baby when he left there. He didn't really have any one place that he called home. He was from all over the place – Jesus of the streets.

2. A Girl of Sixteen

Mama Shenice had it all going on. The way she tells it – and I don't doubt her for a second - she was as beautiful as beautiful can be: a young Nubian Queen of Sheba with a world of flowery ideas and long-considered plans filling her up. She was a bouncing, bubbling up little girl and a bright young lady: an African queen. When Shenice was little, she used to go down to the riverside, sit on a blanket, stare up at the clouds by the hour and see giant ships and trains and rockets that'd help her escape. She was looking for that better life that she'd heard about in school, had read about in books, and had seen on TV. She loved the Bible story of how God got the slaves out of Egypt and she prayed to get out of Harrisburg. But, she was only sixteen; nothing could have prepared her for what happened in the spring of 1979. Shenice had no explanation that made any sense about what happened but she wasn't the first and wouldn't be the last to go tellin' tales once she found out that she was going to have a baby.

3. A Big African Angel

Shenice broke the news to everyone that she was pregnant. She told everyone she'd had a dream and a mysterious messenger came down on her one night and announced that she would soon have a special little baby boy. When she woke up, near sunrise, she went to the restroom and noticed that the bathroom window was open. She felt the bracing chill of the night air and heard the first cries of a few birds. When she closed that window and turned around, there he was – a huge African *angel* standing right in the hallway.

Shenice was naked and so afraid that she couldn't find any air to scream out for help. The big angel told Shenice that he wouldn't hurt her and she shouldn't be afraid. He had been sent from Almighty God to bless her. The big black angel seemed courteous enough. That helped Shenice because she'd never seen any kind of angel before. Still, it sure was awkward to have a divine being in your house while you're plumb naked. Before she could do anything, Shenice felt calmness come over her like a smothering blanket. She closed her eyes and opened her legs. What happened next was that the holy *shadow of the angel came over her.* A second later the angel was gone and she was alone.

When Shenice told her folks she was shocked that they didn't believe her because it'd happened to her as sure as she was Shenice Richardson. Oh sure, they believed that she was pregnant but not in any way that they'd never heard about before. When they got up in her face, she quoted some words she read in the Bible: *"My soul glorifies the Lord and my spirit exults with joy in God, my savior, because He's looked with humility on His handmaid. And from now on, May all generations call me blessed because the Almighty One, whose name is Holy, has worked great things inside of my body."*

When other folks heard this story – and her version spread like wildfire through Harrisburg Central – they said she'd been raped by a zodiac spirit from some unnamed star. One guy joked that she must've been attacked by some monster eagle looking to have a human baby. Others laughed and said she'd probably allowed herself to be raped by some intruder who drugged her to imagine angels and oceans.

Most folks assumed the girl had a boy and was too ashamed to tell her church-folk parents so she had made up her wild story about angels. Kind folks want to believe tall tales. Every wise old mama seems to know that when little girls take to dreaming what they come up with in their imaginations is so outlandish that it almost makes some sense after all. A girl in love for the first time is like an unopened box of fresh ice-cream. Who knows what kind of lofty imaginings such a young girl is capable of?

A neighbor a few houses down – her future sister-in-law – Claire Scott had no problem believing the story as Shenice told it. She convinced everyone else in her family that Shenice had actually been visited by an African Angel. Why not? God can make the world in seven days. Why can't He visit a young girl in Harrisburg with an angel for seven seconds and fashion a little baby boy out of the air? Claire Scott herself was having a baby in a few months and no one knew who the daddy of that child was either. Maybe that's why Claire found the whole story so plausible. Anyway, nine months after the visitation Shenice Richardson delivered a little baby boy into the world.

4. Journey without A Map

Shenice Catherine Richardson was a pregnant girl of 16 who dropped out of the eleventh grade at John Harris High School in Harrisburg, Pennsylvania. These are the cold facts of the story for those of us who've never been a 16-year-old pregnant girl. Everything changed and everyone changed around her. It felt like she lived in a different world and that she was inside of herself alongside the growing little baby. She envied the child because he might grow up and not have to drop out of school or deal with disappointing faces and sarcastic words. She felt like she'd been abandoned on the dark side of the moon with no hope of getting back to the way things were only a month before.

Go ahead and judge her and announce she should've stayed in school - shoulda, coulda, woulda. Everyone gave Shenice their opinions, but none of them were her and no one seemed to believe in her anymore. She felt like a Christmas tree a month after Christmas. Shenice dropped out of school because she needed every ounce of her energy to come back to her own life and find some way forward. That ruled out school. No more English composition and African-American Literature courses, no more American history or science or math, and no more hopes for a college degree to escape into the rich suburbs on the West Shore. She was reduced; just a pregnant, unwed teen - another statistic in a big book that white folks wrote about how black kids get on the wrong side of life too early to recover.

Before the baby, Shenice was just one person. Afterwards – as a mother to be, she was someone else like an alien transformed. Folks talked about her in the past tense. They said that she use to have a way about her. They spoke to the ceiling and remembered how she could cut a rug and step with the best of them when someone turned up M. J. on the radio.

Shenice looked into the mirror. It was her judge, jury, and executioner. Nothing had changed and yet, everything had changed. She was still Shenice. Her wide, beautiful round face looked back at her in the mirror. She looked deep into warm black eyes like a person looks over a stranger at a club for the first time. She touched her fuzzy fro, which made her feel happy; she always loved her hair over any other person's in her family. Have you known a woman who wanted someone else's hair? That was never Shenice. Her hair was who she was. She loved her hair like a cat loves a warm saucer of fresh milk.

Before the pregnancy, Shenice had been getting all A's and B's and everybody talked about how she was going to make a boatload of money someday and be able to take care of her parents when they were in their old age. Nobody said anything like that anymore. Now, folks looked at her as if she was a stranger. They talked to her with a distant, feeble voice as if it was only a courtesy. Shenice remembered specific situations where the comments that her parents used to say about her grades and her plans and went back to the very spots where she'd remembered hearing them like a bird returns to where they'd once found some food. She felt wrapped up like a mummy and desperately wanted to leave Harrisburg.

Even her big dreams were beginning to fade like a tired runner near the end of a long marathon. It used to be at the dinner table that she'd chatter to her folks about how one day she'd go to veterinary school. One day she'd become Dr. Doolittle and live on a big farm down by Gettysburg or someplace and own a horse, donkey, rooster, pig, dog, and cat. She might even own a few goats and sell them to the Mexicans and Africans to eat for their festivals. She never said anything like that anymore at the table. Was this what death felt like? Shenice knew that she hadn't been in a car-wreck or had developed a deadly disease but she felt like her future was already dead.

It was even worse at school. Before she dropped out, Shenice had been popular at John Harris. Once her friends found out that she was pregnant everything changed. As a freshman she'd made the National Honor Society. Because she was such a good dancer and so pretty, talkative, and smart, a lot of the best catches would follow her around the halls. Once her pregnancy began to show, however, she turned into a vampire coming out of a cave or a cop breaking into a crack house looking for people to handcuff. She couldn't wait for school to end in the first week of June. There were no secrets: everybody knew and everybody talked. She had done the same when it was other girls.

5. James Lemiel Scott

In the middle of her mess, and with everything up in the air, Shenice noticed James Lemiel Scott. JL thought that Shenice was incredibly pretty and he'd heard that she was as smart as a brain surgeon. He was older, 26, and lived three or four doors up from the Richardson house. The two of them had joked around from time to time, but since he was so much older, she'd never gave him much mind and just thought of him as a nice church-going person. She liked the fact that he wasn't a party freak, stayed clean, and that he dressed nice. JL had been a good student at John Harris before going to the Harrisburg Area Community College to study business. He'd never had a steady girlfriend which led some folks to joke that he might be gay. When other kids wanted to play for the Sixers or become famous recording artists, JL dreamed of owning his own restaurant. He loved to cook and found steady work in restaurants and hotels all over Harrisburg while studying business at H. A. C. C.

JL had always kept an eye out for Shenice once she started to blossom out about two years before. He noticed that he'd even get a little nervous around her; and he liked that feeling. He didn't see too much of her, but went out of his way to walk by her house or knock on the Richardson door to ask if anybody needed anything when he was going to the grocery.

One night JL heard that Shenice would be at one of her friends' house party. He went there and asked Shenice for a dance when a song from Chaka Khan came on. Shenice had just turned 16, but it was before she had become pregnant and was still the center of attention on the dance floor. JL pulled her in close to him and told her later that she'd set him on fire when he felt her warm, ripe pillows up against his chest.

Once Shenice got pregnant, those same full pillows got even fuller, and that was just all right with JL. When he heard about her pregnancy, he bought her a small porcelain angel and told her how happy he was for her. That was weird. And because he started to hang around the house, folks began to talk that he must've been the father because none of the other boys were coming around anymore. Shenice kept insisting on telling the story about the big African angel who'd given her the baby.

6. West to Pittsburgh

Mr. and Mrs. Richardson didn't feel happy about any of this. The whole thing was getting out of hand. There was too much talking going on in whispers all around them. Folks even began to blame them and their pastor preached a sermon about how parents shouldn't let their children fall into sin because of their own careless and sinful ways. Mama and Papa were devout Christian folks and they never imagined that such a shame would come to them from their own child. Folks also began to talk at work and say things that neither of them wanted to hear about how sad it was that their daughter would probably not make it to a big life and a big job anymore.

It was around the same time, about her fourth month, that Shenice began to show. Once the school year ended, Mrs. Richardson's sister in Pittsburgh called her and suggested that a change would be good for everyone. Shenice was welcome to spend a few months with her until the baby was born.

Her parents hoped that maybe a change would encourage Shenice to stop her lies and finally tell them what had actually happened. Her lying was one of the things that bothered her parents the most because they'd always stressed honesty to their kids. Why couldn't she just tell them the truth? Shenice had always told the truth; neither of them remembered even one instance where she hadn't been entirely honest with them. It was embarrassing. At least if Shenice had made a mistake she should step forward and tell everyone what'd happened so that her parents could speak with the boy's parents and sort this out the way these things had always been dealt with in the past. They asked the girl why she persisted in her fairy tales that only insulted their intelligence and embarrassed them no end.

Mama Richardson had doubts about Shenice going to Pittsburgh. Papa, however, thought it would be best for the girl to go to Aunt Marion's house *for her own good*. At least no one would know her there except her own family. Shenice could get a fresh start. In contrast, Harrisburg was small and nobody forgot anything – especially wild stories like this girl was telling. Aunt Marion promised Shenice that she'd be able to find a few house cleaning jobs for her. Later things would calm down and she could come back home once her baby got on its feet. She could earn some money, take the GED, and maybe go back to school and get some kind of training. She might even find a nice man in Pittsburgh. At least, Shenice would be with family; she wasn't going to some shelter for unwed pregnant drop-out moms.

7. Aunt Marion and Uncle Sam

Aunt Marion and Uncle Sam lived in Pittsburgh about five hours away from Harrisburg by bus. When it was time to leave, there was no party or no big sendoff. The decision was announced on Friday night. She was on the road Saturday. It was the end of August. School had already started without her back at John Harris. Shenice didn't have time to speak with James, but she did ask her oldest sister to tell him where she was going and to give to him Aunt Marion's address where she'd be staying. She took the little porcelain angel he'd given her in her suitcase. It made her feel happy just to look at it.

Papa took her to the Greyhound bus station early on a warm Saturday morning. He gave her a hug, a sack lunch for later, and $20 to "get her started." Shenice packed an old suitcase with clothes, her stuffed animals and dolls, and some family pictures. One of her brothers gave her a Snickers bar for later if she got hungry on the bus. For some reason she'd also packed two novels – *Her Eyes were Watching God* and *Requiem for a Dream*. Shenice loved to read. She felt like she escaped into another world whenever she was in the middle of a good novel. She also took another book – *Apaloochee Red* - along to read on the bus. It was a cool story about a beautiful young Black girl who had a baby with a rich guy in the South who was already married. The boy was born with red hair and that's how the story got its name. The man sent the boy away but Apaloochee came back years later to get his revenge by seducing one of the man's daughters.

The trip seemed strange and exciting to her; she didn't feel afraid at all. She thought that she might've been and her mother had worried out loud the night before that she was too young to travel alone all the way to Pittsburgh. Papa reassured Mama by saying that both Aunt Marion and Uncle Sam would be waiting for her at the big station at the end of Liberty Avenue. There was nothing at all to worry about since there was nothing between home and Pittsburgh anyway.

The night before the family had laid hands on her in a circle of prayer and asked God to protect and bless Shenice and the baby on the way. Some of the other younger kids in the house didn't seem to quite understand what was going on with their big sister. It was one of the prayers that you weren't exactly sure if it was a prayer to God in heaven above or a prayer to each other to get a message across to those listening in the circle - if you know what I mean.

Going on that bus to Pittsburgh was the farthest she'd ever traveled in her life. One time before, she'd been to Philadelphia to see relations with her family which was a little more than two hours driving. Another time, she went with some of her friends to Hershey, but that was less than an hour away. Hershey's Chocolate Town had this wonderful train you went on that showed you how chocolate was made and being on their little chocolate train made her feel as if nothing was wrong with the world.

The bus trip to Pittsburgh took its sweet old time. Shenice looked out the window through all of those hours of green fields. She felt relaxed. It would've been nice to have a few days and just wander up and down those fields if the farmers wouldn't mind. Since it was the end of August some of the farmers were beginning to harvest their crops. Shenice watched them with envy. She had no idea about how long she'd be staying at Auntie Marion's but she felt like everything was in God's hands like her Mama had told her that morning when she kissed her at the doorway of their home. She didn't worry either about only having one suitcase and only a few light clothes. Auntie Marion had told her when they had talked on the phone that she'd be able to get some winter clothes from the South Hills Interfaith Ministry clothing office so not to bring too much along in the bus. It'd all work out.

Auntie Marion took Shenice in like a stray polecat out of the kindness of her heart. Anyway, she'd always liked the girl. It wasn't like Marion and Sam was rich but they paid their bills on time (or close to it) and always had a little extra to spare for a few small treats. Even though their house was small, nobody made Shenice feel like she was intruding. Shenice even had a room of her own. She didn't have to share it with anyone. It was so nice to just retreat into her little room and stare up at the ceiling in the same way that she had used to stare up at the clouds along the riverbank. She also liked the fact that the phone was right outside her bedroom so she could talk privately with James if he ever called.

Uncle Sam and Auntie Marion Richardson lived with their only daughter Kinetra, in Coverdale, Bethel Park, which is about ten miles outside of Pittsburgh and is a small town built on an abandoned coal mine. Coverdale was one of those places that was kinda hidden away from the whites in the town. You might not even know that it was there unless you made a wrong turn behind the post office or the Twin-Kiss ice-cream store. Auntie's house was full of noise and life. Kinetra was about 22 and had an 8 month old baby boy of her own named Marcus. The house was always full of plenty of crazy noise. Aunt Marion joked that there was always room for a few more noise-makers.

Bethel Park was a nice area. There was a large public park nearby where she could walk around a little. At this park they even had a herd of buffalo which was something more exotic than Shenice could imagine. The place was called South Park and it seemed to Shenice like the Garden of Eden. She liked to imagine which of the trees in that big park was the Tree of Good and Evil - with the apple and the snake that she remembered Mama talking about when she was a little girl. The location of Coverdale was also pretty decent when it came to moving around. There were both trolley and bus lines from there into the city. It would not be too hard for her to get around once she figured out the routes.

The section of Coverdale that Auntie Marion lived in was called *The Bricks*. It was not much to speak of. People who didn't know better - and looking at the house from the outside - might say that it was dilapidated - unsanitary and unsafe. A passerby might have thought that the house should be condemned if anyone in the local township was actually paying any attention. Nobody had any extra money to throw into landscaping or anything like that. But Auntie Marion and Uncle Sam had made a warm home of the place and, to them, it felt like a castle. Auntie filled the house to the brim with knickknacks and all kinds of furniture. She used to collect little black angels and also found some little German houses in a garage sale once so she mixed the angels in with the German scene to make her own little world where nothing bad ever would happen. There was hardly room in that house to move around since it was so filled with stuff. Auntie Marion was a pack rat. One of the things that she also did was to buy a number of paintings for the walls from the Salvation Army of river scenes and wooded wonderlands. The way Mama Shenice described it to me that little house sure must've been filled to the brim with Auntie Marion's heart of warm love and attention.

Remember I said it was noisy? The loudest thing in the house was not Kinetra's crying baby, but it was Auntie Marion's beloved parrot *Rory* who squawked from morning 'til night. Uncle Sam hated that bird and often went out to drink at a shady local bar for men-only called *Tennyson's* because, as he said, he didn't need to come home to an angry parrot, a lazy daughter, a baby grandson, and a complaining wife after dealing with white folks all day at the Virgili's Beer Distributor at the edge of Coverdale. To make matters worse, baby Marcus was always sick and Kinetra was always gone either to her community college classes - which took more than an hour to get to on the bus - or to hang out with her friends in the downtown clubs. Auntie Marion did the best she could to keep some order in the house. It wasn't easy.

Auntie Marion worked in the public library and, true to her promise, was able to find a bit of house-cleaning work for Shenice. The idea was for her to help out a little with the rent and also begin to save a little for the future once the baby arrived. Living here was a good experience for Shenice. No one asked her questions or gave her any grief. She soon fit into the routine of helping to clean the house and cook dinners for Auntie Marion while she was at work. She began to feel the baby heavier and heavier and felt more and more tired every day. Whenever she did go and clean a house, it seemed like it took her forever to finish.

When she wasn't cleaning someone's house she loved to cook because it was something she had never really done before at her Mama's house. The first burnt offerings that she made weren't much to speak of, but Auntie was patient with her. It wasn't long before she began teaching Shenice some of the local specialties of Pittsburgh that she'd never imagined that she'd be eating in a million months of Sundays. It seemed that Uncle Sam's favorite dinner was kielbasa and sauerkraut with a plateful of potato, cheese, and onion pierogies. Shenice had never even seen these weird foods before. She remembered that a friend of her mother's, Squirrel Moseley, used to make sauerkraut with pork but she'd never even heard of kielbasa. Shenice said that that woman was an excellent cook, too. Shenice said she was at her home many an evening saying "Amen" at the dinner blessing.

8. JL Joins Shenice in the Steel City

When Shenice got to Pittsburgh, she talked to her Mama on the phone every day for the first week. Nobody else, however, tried to reach her or send her a letter. There was only one exception: JL called her every other day and wrote her once a week. He said that he was praying for Shenice every day. Most of all, Shenice liked their phone conversations because he asked questions about how she was feeling. He was the only person who'd ever asked her about her moods. He listened. Soon she knew that JL not only believed in her, but also that he was in love with her. It wasn't long before JL told her that he was going to come to Pittsburgh so he could be closer to her. He joked that he'd save just as much money on postage and phone calls as if he rented an apartment. Truth be told; he also was looking for some fresh adventures away from the predictable day-to-day of life in Harrisburg.

JL heard about a friend whose uncle worked in Pittsburgh. That uncle promised JL a steady job with plenty of hours at a big hotel. In mid-September, James Scott left Harrisburg and took a position at the Hilton Hotel at the Point State Park in downtown Pittsburgh as a banquet waiter. The folks back in Harrisburg; especially Shenice's parents, learned of his decision as the final confirmation they were looking for to show that JL had been the father of the child and that he'd been the one who had taken advantage of this innocent young girl with his older, sneaky ways.

When JL got to Pittsburgh he went right to work the very same day. The plan was to stay with his friend's uncle until he got his first paycheck. Then he was going to find a room somewhere closer to Shenice in the South Hills. The catering gig was awesome for a young kid from a small town. JL had plenty of hours. He had a decent enough boss -- Tommy O'Reiley -- and got paid every two weeks. It wasn't unusual to work ten hours and when they had a wedding banquet or something it was even more hours; it was perfect work for JL. As an extra plus, the Hilton Hotel was one of the most well-known hotels in the city. All kinds of famous folks showed up at the restaurant when they came into Pittsburgh. It was in the "Golden Triangle" and just across the street from the fourth-river fountain of the old Point State Park where JL would sometimes go on his breaks. From time to time, working at the Hilton JL would have the chance to host some of the Steelers and some of the other NFL teams that used the Hilton's catering services when they came through town to get beaten up and crushed under the tough Steel curtain. He thought everyone in the Steeler nation should make the pilgrimage to Pittsburgh at least once in their lifetimes if they were physically able and could afford it.

After his first paycheck, JL found a small room to rent in a Pittsburgh neighborhood called Homewood-Brushton. There sure weren't any white folks living in that neighborhood. Homewood-Brushton wasn't as close to Shenice as he'd hoped but it was much closer than he'd been before. It was also more convenient for him in terms of getting into work every day on the bus. He had made friends with a man at work, LaVar Arrington who lived there and LaVar helped him to find the room and even gave JL a few sticks of furniture.

JL finally felt like a real man. He felt responsible and was proud when he walked into his own apartment for the first time and realized how far he'd come since his days in Harrisburg. And, it was all because JL took a step to be closer to Shenice. Life sure has its ways of twisting and turning whenever love gets into the picture doesn't it? Why not risk it all because who knows when a person will die anyway. It can happen in a moment just when you're walkin' down the street so you might as well take some chances. Actually, it really wasn't that hard at all for JL to leave Harrisburg. He felt like he was on a pilgrimage. JL didn't know much but he knew that he wanted to marry this sweet and sassy woman named Shenice. He wanted to help her make it in life even though he knew that her baby was not his.

9. Betrothal

Auntie Marion invited JL to dinner. He decided to make his big move on Shenice after the meal. The meal went on forever and the food was like heaven on earth. Auntie Marion must've been cooking for a week to make all of that food and it was no small wonder that the table just didn't crash to the ground under the weight of all of her food.

JL decided to ask Shenice to marry him right after her baby was born. Who knew when that'd be because Shenice was already into her eighth month. For some reason, JL's proposal surprised her but without blinking an eye she said yes. Shenice didn't jump up and kiss him like he'd hoped but at least he was on the way. Her response was matter-of-fact as if she was responding to some question on a form. That didn't matter to JL. He was the happiest man in the world. That little house in Coverdale was the most holy place in the world to him in that moment.

Everything was happening so fast for Shenice. She felt like she was in the middle of a whirlwind while trying to ride the back of a hungry tiger. The move to a big city, the exhausting pregnancy, and her new boyfriend – now her fiancé – all seemed overwhelming. Everything had gotten very complicated. All Shenice wanted to do was just to sleep and get through another day in one piece.

In the summer, Kinetra had advised Shenice not to follow her own example of being a young mother but to get an abortion and then get on with her life. Kinetra talked about how tired she always was as a young mama. She talked about how it was hard for her to have any fun or do anything she wanted 'cause her kid was like a chain around her leg dragging her down into more work and less fun. Other people back in Harrisburg had told her the same thing when she first learned she was pregnant. Shenice didn't really care about having fun or going to parties or even working or travelling or all of that. At this point, there was no turning back. She was way too many months along. Right after she got to Pittsburgh in the summer, Kinetra even walked Shenice into an abortion clinic - without warning her where they were going - to make an appointment. Once Shenice figured out where she was – after about five minutes in a crowded waiting room – she ran out the door. Her mind was made up. She wanted to be a Mama just like her own Mama and every other woman she knew. Shenice had already felt her own little baby kicking inside of her.

10. House-Cleaning in Brookside Farms, December 24, 1979

Right before Christmas, Shenice had an appointment to clean the house of a rich white lady, a Miss Erika Lutsch, in Bethel Park who was having some kind of a big German Christmas party. Miss Erika was not a regular house for her but she'd been recommended to Miss Erika through Auntie Marion who met the white woman at the library. When Mama Shenice told me about this I asked her what she meant by a "German Christmas Party." She said it was when German people would have actual candles burning on their Christmas trees, when they'd would eat a lot of black bread and ham, and drink a lot of wine and sing German carols and stuff like that.

Shenice had never cleaned in Brookside before. She did clean a few houses in Oakhurst – she worked once a week for Miss Gianni, for Mrs. Manning, and for Mr. Dave and for his teenage daughter Kate. Most of her houses, however, were much further away from Coverdale. But, even though they were further away, they were actually easier to get to most of the time because of the trolley. Normally, Shenice could take a Shannon Library trolley to Mount Lebanon or someplace to do her cleaning jobs. This house, however, was on the Drake line; not the Library line. It'd take her almost an hour to walk there at her pace. Every step was a major accomplishment. She had no choice. She needed the money.

To make matters worse after Shenice was walking awhile it began to drizzle a soft rain. It was also about forty degrees: miserable weather. Since it was a neighborhood there was really no place to go for cover and the best idea seemed to just hurry up as best as she could and just get it over with. While she was walking Shenice wondered if it'd even crossed Miss Erika's mind when she'd asked Auntie Marion to find someone to work for her that she might also offer to give them a ride or ask if that was a problem. Maybe once she got there she could ask Miss Erika to call Uncle Sam to drive and pick her up from there once he got off of work so she wouldn't have to do all this same walking again. The weather seemed to be getting worser and worser by the minute. For Shenice, every step up that steep hill on Kennebec Road seemed to weigh her and her baby down. It seemed like her legs were sledgehammers being driven hard into the ground. She was very big and just plain exhausted all the time. As she was walking, Shenice decided that this would probably have to be the last job that she'd agree to take until after her baby was born. It all felt so weird. She felt like she was a small boat or a big circus tent on two legs. As she strained uncomfortably toward her work she felt her baby kicking away more strongly than ever. It was like her baby was fighting off a pack of hounds inside her belly.

After what seemed like forever, Shenice finally reached the big house – all the way up Kennebec and down to the corner of Apache. Miss Erika opened the door. She offered Shenice a cup of coffee which was nice of her but all Shenice wanted to do was to get her directions about what she needed to do and get on with it so she could get home as soon as she possibly could. Soon enough, after she got to Miss Erika's house, things began to happen. After about ten minutes of cleaning with the Windex, she began to feel deep cramps.

Shenice started to feel dizzy like she was drunk. But, she had no choice but to go on working and hoping that she could get home once Uncle Sam got off of work. She hoped, this was just one of those spells she had had before which would pass in a few minutes. Every breath took so much effort. Things started to turn upside down. She felt like she was being ripped apart like one of those wrecking balls digs into an abandoned building or one of those claws does to an old car at the junkyard. This was something new: All she could think to do was to pray and to keep on walking forward. *Thank you Jesus- Thank you Jesus – Thank you Jesus* she prayed with every slower step.

It was happening. What should she do now? There was no time to make any kind of plan that made any sense. Shenice had no health insurance. She had no money to pay for an ambulance and Uncle Sam was still at work. She knew that JL wasn't working yet. She saw the phone in Miss Erika's basement and she called JL. She felt like she was being eaten up by that big python called childbirth. When he picked up Shenice managed to tell JL to get on the first trolley he could find on the Shannon Drake line and get himself at the second to the last stop on the line over to 3239 Apache. JL wrote down the address. She dropped the phone. JL ran out of work at the Hilton right away without saying boo to anybody. He knew it'd take at least an hour to get there.

Shenice then yelled as best as she could up the basement steps to tell Miss Erika that she might need help. It felt strange that she needed the help of a stranger so much at this the most important moment in her life but there was nobody else for her. As soon as Miss Erika started to come down the steps to the basement, Shenice doubled over in pain and gave out a loud scream that seemed to rip the heavens into two with its shrill siren call. The older white woman hurried down the steps seemingly just in time to catch Shenice's flailing arms. Miss Erika lovingly helped her as best as she could but there wasn't much that she really could do except pick up the phone and call for an ambulance.

At that very instant Shenice's water broke; rivers of living water were all over the basement floor. She went to her knees in the middle of the puddle while Miss Erika held her and told her that it would all be all right; an ambulance would soon be here for her. There was blood. What was happening to Shenice was nothing like anything that'd ever happened to her before. The pain told her that the world was coming to an end and that Jesus was coming back to the earth to take us all to heaven in a cloud of glory. She felt like she was being ripped into two rough pieces by a sharp, noisy chainsaw.

Shenice was being stabbed inside of herself with sharp knitting needles. There was nothing she could do to stop the burning thrusts of the pain after pain. She was being dragged down a country road on an unbreakable iron chain behind a pickup truck of laughing Klansmen. She was dizzy, hot, thirsty, and dry, tired, and sick all at the same time. She felt sicker than sick. All Shenice had time to do before exploding like a suicide bomber was to call out to the wonder-working name of the Lord Jesus Christ.

The baby came quickly right after the ambulance guy arrived. It seemed like only a few minutes at the time but who knows how long the thrusts lasted before the baby came out. Miss Erika was able to get some towels once the ambulance guy held on to Shenice. Shenice vaguely heard a voice telling her to lean against the wall and push. All Shenice could do was moan and sweat and nod at Miss Erika's directions as she pushed the child out into the world. Right then and there, the battle finally ended.

Neither Shenice nor Miss Erika said much of anything at that point – maybe because they were both so surprised. The ambulance guy was rushing around. They got a stretcher and put Shenice on it with the baby in her arms.

The only thing Miss Erika could say was "What a beautiful little chocolate baby." Shenice smiled and stared into the baby's warm deep eyes. The baby cried and that pushed Miss Erika into a next-step mode. She ran into the laundry room next to the basement where they were and pulled out one of her son's Steelers jerseys to wrap around the newborn to keep him warm in the cold air.

A second ambulance person – probably the driver – joined his friend and they lifted Shenice into the ambulance. One of the ambulance workers checked her heartbeat after he shut the door. They drove away, sirens blaring. Shenice held a little brown package of wet skin, black eyes, and tiny little baby hands. The ambulance guy dipped some scissors into some cleaning solution and then expertly cut the baby's cord. He checked out both the mother and child. The ambulance seemed so warm.

Miss Erika followed the ambulance to the Magee Women's Hospital in her brand new Plymouth Horizon. It was about a forty-five minute drive to the hospital without the help of ambulance sirens but that way it seemed like it only took about thirty minutes. What a parade. Shenice felt like she was somebody special. She imagined all of the cars pulling aside to let her fly by like a royal queen. Miss Erika was able to stay up with the ambulance and stay right with Shenice and her baby when they got to Magee. While Shenice plopped down into a cold plastic orange chair with her baby Miss Erika tried to plead with the nurses at the desk to get them into a warm room.

At first, things were slow since it was Christmas Eve. They had to wait for awhile in a really cold waiting room before someone could find Shenice and the baby boy a bed. The wait was horrible because the waiting room was right by an automatic door into the underground parking lot. Every time the door opened it let in another sharp, cold blast of shocking air that hit them like a ton of bricks.

It'd been drizzling all day and now it was nighttime. You could also smell the exhaust from the cars when they were parking. It seemed like an hour, but finally somebody got her and the baby into a room and the doctor came and checked out the vitals of the mother and child. Everything was okay for both of them.

The room that they finally got checked into felt more like a closet or a High School gym locker more than it did a full room. Maybe this was because she had no insurance. To make matters worse, Shenice and the baby were sharing the room with another lady. What bothered Shenice about this was it seemed like other people in the waiting room had been admitted before she was and now it even seemed like this other lady in her room was getting much more attention than she was. The feeling of being a queen had long since taken flight. All Shenice wanted to do now was survive. She wanted to get out of there and get home to JL and Auntie Marion and everybody and show them her little baby boy.

Shenice was so tired and happy and exhausted and amazed at herself all at once. It felt like her heart was struck at by a thousand different arrows from all directions. The baby was as real as real could be. It had happened. It wasn't a dream. The baby cried a little. His skin was dark-dark: darker than a thousand midnights down in the bayou.

11. Naming the Baby

JL had been thinking for months about what he wanted to name the little boy if Shenice ever asked him for his opinion on that subject. The conversation never came up. That was probably for the best and maybe that's why Shenice never asked. JL had hoped that Shenice would allow him to name the boy Wilver Dornell Stargell Scott in honor of the great star of the World Champion Pittsburgh Pirates. Dornell sure seemed like a name for fit for a king somewhere over in England or someplace while Willie seemed to sound like somebody who cut your hair and knew you all of your life so the combination of the two names sounded just perfect to JL.

JL had met the hulking monster of a Bucco superstar one evening out of the blue while he was catering at the Hilton. It had been after one of the games. Sure enough, just like the legend about him goes, Willie ate what seemed like a bucketful of chicken that night but JL insisted on paying for Stargell's dinner. Willie didn't accept the offer which made JL even more of a fan. Lord, that baseball man sure could eat – and he could hit a ball a good country mile as well. JL thought that he and Willie could've probably been good friends if given half the chance. The man seemed to have a heart of gold. He tipped a godly twenty percent.

JL had always been a huge baseball fan growing up. He had come to town just as the Pirates "Fam-a-lee" were trying to win the World Series against the vaunted Orioles of Baltimore. Even though the Bucs had beaten the ferocious Reds to get this far it almost seemed like they were up against a wall too high. Those Orioles had everything that year, Nobody was gonna get in their way. It was almost like Godzilla going against King Kong and here JL was right in the middle of the fight. He knew he wasn't in Harrisburg now! The Hilton was buzzing like a hornet's nest the whole time the 1979 Major League Baseball World Series was going on. It was one of the happiest times of his life.

JL had to work during the Sunday night game –game five and he watched the game – along with everybody else – at the TV at the Hotel Bar. At the start of the game the owl-faced announcer, Howard Cosell, told everyone that Coach Tanner's mom had died that morning. Everyone in the bar-room seemed to feel like it was their own mother who'd died. Mother of God! One thing was sure, the Pirates sure needed a miracle or they were about to be knocked off. Not a whole lot of work got done that night at the Hilton but nobody seemed to care. The crowd was loose and loud. There were flags everywhere and a guy named Jim Rooker kept it close until ace Bert Blyleven could finish off the Orioles and help the Bucs to a do-or-die victory. That gangly white guy Blyleven was called the Dutchman. For some reason he always reminded JL of the timid lion in the Wizard of Oz. That World Series time was fun: JL couldn't wait to get to work to see who might walk into his restaurant at the hotel.

The 1979 Pittsburgh Pirates called themselves the "Fam-a-lee" after the Sister Sledge song which they'd taken on as their motto in the clubhouse to get them all motivated and united. It was them against the world. They had a catcher named Sanguillen who would smile in the middle of a crocodile attack. They had a right fielder, number 39, named the Cobra. How is that for a terrifying name!

The Bucs had some great pitching – the Candy Man and a guy named Kent Tekulve who looked like a mad scientist when he pitched. One of their best pitchers was named Doc Ellis. This guy once even pitched a no hitter when he was strung out on drugs. That sure wouldn't have been all that easy to do I'd guess. The Pittsburgh Pirates had a great lineup but nobody was better on their team than the old veteran Pops; "Chicken-on-the-Hill-with-Will," Willie Stargell. Every time Stargell hit one of his towering blast

Homeruns that what the Gunner - Bob Prince, the old Southern radio man for the Pirates, used to yell out "there-goes-Chicken-on-the-hill-with-Will" and every time the Gunner said it, JL felt so happy.

The best thing about the Gunner was that he would always tell long stories and jokes that had nothing to do with the game. Sometimes his stories had nothing at all to do with modern times. Shenice told me a story that JL had told her over and over again about the 1924 World Series when some guy named Walter Big Train Johnson beat the Pirates in Pittsburgh. He won even though the groundskeepers kept putting water on the pitcher's mound before he went to pitch and then put dirt on the pitcher's mound for the Buccos to dry it off. She also told me a story about a baseball player named Ty Cobb. Some sports journalist in the early 60s asked the old-timer Cobb what he would hit if he was playing in the Majors now since there were new rules, more games, a watered-down league and other advantages. Cobb answered that he would probably only hit about .270 or .280. When the sports writer was surprised at the modest answer Ty Cobb responded by saying: "Hell, I'm 68 years old!"

For JL it was great to be in Pittsburgh and be able to look out and see Three Rivers Stadium from the Point State Park Hilton while he was working and watch the place light up for games. In the winter the stadium would light up like a holy cathedral for the Steeler games. I guess football is more like a religion than a game for the people who live in that part of the country.

The first time the idea of what to call the baby came up it was JL who mentioned it. It was right after he proposed to her at Thanksgiving and he said it to her kinda like it was a joke. Shenice, however, was no baseball fan and didn't think it was a very funny idea to name her kid Wilver Dornell Stargell Scott. She didn't give JL's idea the time of day. In fact, she made sure that she thought he was joking with him and that was her way of laying down the law. Of course, she did want to honor JL by giving him his last name. Since they'd be married soon anyway that would be a good thing for the baby to have on his birth certificate.

Since the baby ended up being born on Christmas Eve she felt even a little more power to tell the nurse at the hospital the name for the child that she'd picked out but that she knew might turn some heads: The birth certificate for her son was to read *Jesus Dred Scott.*

Shenice chose the middle name *Dred* because of Dred Scott that she had heard about in her African American literature class at John Harris High. She always liked that name and when she met JL and found out his last name was "Scott" it was one of the first things she said to him: *"Ahh, like in Dred Scott?"*

JL had actually never heard about Dred Scott before. When he asked his sister Catherine he felt a little better because she'd never heard about him either. The literature teacher had told Shenice's class about this man – Dred Scott- who had been an escaped slave before the Civil War. The teach said that the story was important because, even though the man claimed the Declaration of Independence said he should be free and was created equal by God Almighty like everybody else, the judge at the trial – Judge Taney- sent the man back to his slave master named John Emerson. Slavery made her so mad even though she couldn't quite explain why it bothered her so much. When she heard the stories of folks like Harriet Tubman and Dred Scott who fought it made her proud. She loved her literature teacher for telling her those stories with such passion. Going to that class and hearing about slavery was like watching a vivid TV soap opera to Shenice. It also made her feel deeply sad and angry at the same time so she thought a lot about the story of Dred Scott.

Why in the world did Shenice chose to give the baby the first name of Jesus? Well, the fact it was Christmas made her feel a little more comfortable about the name but the real reason was that she chose the name *Jesus* for her baby because Christ Jesus was the only person whom she really trusted and felt safe with in her entire life. Sure, he was far away up in heaven and not in America. But the Lord Jesus Christ was a holy man who'd never once let her down. To say the name of Jesus on her lips was to feel love like she was being kissed by an angel. The sound of the name of Jesus was sweeter than honey to her ears. Jesus was the best and she wanted her son to be the best. She also used to tell people that her baby – born on Christmas Eve – was a special Christmas present from God Almighty.

All of her life, Shenice had been one of those folks who'd really loved the Christmas holiday season. She loved Christmas even though, for her, it rarely meant as a kid growing up that she was going to get any special big Christmas presents or something like that. The world around her just felt different then. It felt special. The songs, the lights, the colors, the music, the way church felt at Christmas, her family's Christmas dinner, and the presents they had all made her feel like it was one day in the year that she had won the jackpot or had been set out of a prison for a day to get some fresh air and sunshine.

Her favorite song on the radio was Bing Crosby singing *I'll be Home for Christmas*. Shenice loved how Der Bingle's manly voice made her feel all warm inside. Christmas to Shenice was about belonging and having a home. Time stood still and the clock was turned off. It seemed like no one had any problems to complain about at least on that one day. It was cool to her that one day in the year everything shut down and was closed because of something that had happened two thousand years before.

Besides *I'll be Home for Christmas,* her favorite religious Christmas song was *Silent Night.* She felt like, while Bing Crosby's song touched her heart, that old hymn she heard in church when everyone lit Christmas candles touched her soul and moved in her spirit. Shenice remembered her mother every Christmas meal looking up gratefully to the sky in their home back in Harrisburg and simply saying: *"He dwelt among us. He dwelt among us. He dwelt among us"* as if she was a magician reciting a powerful incantation. That was the theme of the sermon the Pastor in Harrisburg at Wesley Zion always used to present on Christmas day. Mama Shenice said she loved the sound of those four words ever since she was a little girl. When Shenice was little she dreamed that one day she'd have a little baby just like Mary had at Christmas. One day she'd also set down her baby boy into some straw and wrap him into some golden, heavenly swaddling clothes.

Once the baby was named and everyone had gotten some sleep it was Christmas day. But it seemed so different for Shenice than any other Christmas. Auntie Marion and Uncle Sam, and even Kinetra, had gotten to Magee Hospital just as soon as they could after they heard on their message machine from JL what'd happened. Miss Erika stayed at the hospital for a few hours. That kind lady even paid the emergency bill which was a big surprise and a huge relief for Shenice. For some reason, Shenice wondered about one little detail. She wondered if Miss Erika would end up cleaning up her house herself or if she'd cancel her German party.

Later, she asked about this and found out that Miss Erika had gone ahead with her German party-messy house and all. Shenice called her on the phone to thank her and tell her how the baby was doing. Miss Erika said that she had had so much fun telling her guests about all the adventures of the day before. She told them that none other than a black Jesus had been born in her basement. Miss Erika laughed and loved to tell about the name of the baby, a black Jesus, born in her home. Imagine that!

Hearing that bit of news made Shenice happy. Miss Erika being so nice to her made Shenice think that she wanted to learn German someday as some kind of way of repaying that lady for her kind heart and soft way. Shenice felt that God Almighty had worked it all out for her and that

Miss Erika had been some kind of angel who'd brought a healing to her heart about white and rich folks. It was nice to Shenice that her son had a special birth story. Some day he could go to that big house over on Apache Road and ask whoever lived there to look into the basement to see where he'd been born. Shenice imagined the idea of her son doing that with his wife and children someday. The Holy Bible, she remembered, says that we'll all go to a big mansion of gold in the sky when we die. Shenice felt happy that her son had already been born in a big mansion out in the rich suburbs of Pittsburgh.

Whenever someone acted surprised with Mama Shenice about the name of her baby she told them that the name made her happy; that that was all that mattered. She loved her son's name. Some of his friends thought it was weird but I was fine with it. After all, a lot of us Hispanics sometimes call our kids *Jesus* don't we? The titles, honors, and nicknames that we get later we earn – but, our names are a gift from our mothers with all of their love and hope for us at our fresh beginnings. Mama loved to call out his name – Jesus! Shenice spent hours in those first days just holding her baby in her arms and whispering what her mother used to say over and over again at Christmas: *"He dwelt among us."*

12. Genealogy

That first day that he was born the baby Jesus kept crying. He didn't seem to want to sleep. It wouldn't be the first time or the last time that he'd disturb everyone around him without giving up. Because it was Christmastime, McGee was short staffed and nurses were running around everywhere. Another problem was that – and this was all so confusing - because Shenice had no insurance, the hospital had to conjure up some kind of form letter from Miss Erika promising payment before they could release her and before they could check out the baby. When the baby finally fell asleep in the hospital room, Shenice turned to JL and asked him to read for her from the Holy Bible.

You could hear the pounding sleet of an icy rain outside. You could see through the window of the room the city lights twinkling outside of Magee Women's Hospital in Oakland. It was sharply cold and miserable outside but warm and wonderful inside this magical room. The slow sweet spiderweb hours of the first night after anyone has a newborn are impossible to forget. Warm specialness mixes with quiet, exhaustion and the baby sleeps and the parents watch in awe unable to sleep themselves.

Sitting in the little hospital chair JL allowed himself to review recent events: It'd been a long day. He'd left work after Shenice had called and made it all the way from the Point to Miss Erika's house only to find a note taped on the door for him - *"JL – It's a baby boy- We are at Magee Women's Hospital -Mrs. Erika."* JL had just run all the way from the trolley stop in the rain. Now, he had to go all the way back to Magee Women's. He had $20 in his wallet and guessed that that'd be enough for a taxi. There were no trolleys out to Oakland and he had no idea what bus connection he'd need to get out there. He went to the neighbor's house to ask to make a phone call to call a taxi to take him to the hospital.

Minutes passed like hours. Sitting in the room that night after everything had settled down JL began to read a Holy Bible on the hospital room countertop to Shenice as she had requested. He was an excellent reader and prided himself on his diction and reading skill: *"Abraham begot Isaac and Isaac begot Jacob and Jacob begot Judah and his brothers and Judah begot Phares and Zara out of Thamar...."*

The words were reassuring in their meaninglessness and their sense of boredom. There was nothing important about the names; that's why they were comforting. When you read the Holy Bible nobody asked you to pay an unpaid light bill or deal with a problem relative or solve an unsolved problem. The Holy Bible can lift you away from the stress of everybody trying to take something from you. Those long lists of ancient names in the Holy Bible reassured JL that there were connections all around us that hold us up. We were all together in the same boat. None of us were here on our own by ourselves without beginning or end.

Hearing long list of names from the Holy Bible also warmed Shenice. She closed her eyes as she listened: *"Nassan begot Salmon and Salmon begot Boaz out of Rachab and Boaz begot Obed out of Ruth and Obed begot Jesse and Jesse begot King David."* King David was in some kind of all-star lineup as well. The syllables of the names tasted like warmed milk and hot cookies. The heater in the hospital room was turned up to hell-fire boiling. Everything seemed so quiet and all of the begetting in the Holy Bible seemed to hold everything up from falling down all around her.

JL, who'd enjoyed reading the names, noticed that Shenice had her eyes closed. He kept reading because, once when he stopped, she opened her eyes. Life sometimes simply comes down to us feeling comfortable enough to close our eyes. For all of the grandiose notions of travelling to distant countries like Spain or Casablanca, or buying a classic Bugatti, or an old Duisenberg, or having money to give your woman some fine Cartier jewelry, or some Grey Goose Whiskey, happiness can often be all about feeling calm, safe and secure, like the little baby Jesus sleeping motionless on his Mama's breast.

Most of us don't know the list of criminal rogues and holy angels that are in our own genealogies. I bet if I could take a machine back into time that I'd get into fights with half of the DNA that is inside of who I am. A list of names is no way to trace your roots or to learn how you are connected back to people in ancient Mexico or at the Alamo, but maybe it is as good a way as any other. Who knows? Maybe me and some famous painter or some rich baseball players are related? I guess I'll never find out. For me, the memory of my grandma and grandpa's laughter is my connection going back into the distant highways of the past.

One of my friends said that if you want to know about your ancestors you should ask a Mormon because they are really into birth and burial records. Mormons are those white in-bred looking guys in the white shirts and name-tags and with the black pants on bicycles. Those people are way too weird for me to ask them about my ancestors. It's probably one of their traps to get you to join their religion like how somebody offers you a free t-shirt if you sign up for a credit card. A genealogy shows how many people go into making God's plan for us. Each name has stories of a first kiss or a last thought before dying. Maybe one of my ancestors was a gallant soldier or a beautiful senorita with black, silky hair that reached down to the floor. Stories of the old ones held onto the same promises and some of the same hopes that we hold. God Almighty was as trustworthy to them as He now is to us.

God Almighty loves each of us by name. That idea gives me hope that my life will add up to something in the bigger equation. All of us are woven into the fabric of history and into each other's lives. We all come from Adam and Eve and from lofty kings and lowly frog-catchers. I'm sure some of my ancestors were scholars from a castle in Spain and others were illiterates who tried to dodge paying their bills. That last one would not surprise me at all. Everyone, though, can be good at something or know something that somebody else knows nothing about. An illiterate fool isn't someone who can't read but someone who refuses to learn or to create something new.

King David begot Solomon out of the wife of Uriah and Solomon begot Reheboam and Reheboam begot Abijah, and Abijah begot Asa and Asa begot Jehosephet." JL remembered dozing off to the voice of Ed and Wendy King on the Party Line on KDKA radio late at night or the voice of the Gunner and Nellie King when he listened to the Pirates playing their West Coast games. The days, months and years went by, but the lineup didn't really change all that much. Frank Taveras begot Tim Foli, and Tim Foli begot Bill Madlock, and Bill Madlock begot Omar Moreno, and Omar Moreno begot Rene Stennett, who begot Dave Parker, and Dave Parker begot Dock Ellis, and Dock Ellis begot Manny Sanguillen, and Manny Sanguillen begot Wilver Dornell Stargell. He dwelt among us.

JL thought again about the World Champion Buccos. Willie had a way of winding up the bat like a windmill. The World Series against the Baltimore Orioles had been a chance for old Willie to shine on his own out from the shadow of the Great One- Roberto *Bob* Clemente. See, Clemente was a "spic" and so he had to be called "Bob" instead of "Roberto." The voice of Bob Prince used to shout out *Arriba! Arriba!* Whenever the Great One – Clemente - came to bat. The Gunner was much more direct with old Willie and his homeruns that seemed to stretch toward the Allegheny and Monongahela Rivers on their way to one victory after another. Clemente was long gone. He had flown up into the sky but got too close to the sun. He fell to the earth trying to help some people covered up in volcanic lava somewhere down in the middle of all of those poor people in the banana jungles of Central America.

JL would sit in bed at night trying to unwind and then the Gunner would shout out a home- run: *"Have some chicken on the hill with Will."* That was about the perfect time to fall asleep and dream.

The genealogy list in the Holy Bible that JL was reading to Shenice must've had some kind of point at the end of it. He read on while waiting to hear the name Jesus that certainly would come at the end. JL tried his best to take time to pronounce every name and every syllable of every name. He thought about all of that begetting. The long list of goat-herders and kings with their black beards and strange ways and robes; none of them had ever seen a baseball game. All of these names would end up famous with angels in a Bethlehem stable on a long-lost Christmas morning. The men, who once had such pride and power, were now only names. Even so, they were beautiful names- *Jehosephet begot Joram and Joram begat Azariah and Azariah begot Jothan and Jotham begot Ahaz."*

Maybe Shenice was asleep now and JL could stop reading the long list. Some of the names he knew but most seemed so obscure. Some of them were probably murderers or some of them were men who cheated on their wives. Yet, here they were in this list made significant by an unforeseen little poor baby at the end of their lineup. Every one of their lives, their failures, and their successes moved humanity one step closer to the one they'd all been waiting for. From this entire mysterious network comes one: *"Matthan begot Jacob and Jacob begot Joseph the husband of Mary."* And suddenly, the list was over. There was no Jesus. Why? Who did Joseph beget?

13. Hospital Visitors

Mama Shenice tapped her feet and sang along to the music being played lowly over the hospital speakers. She knew all of the words of every single Christmas song. These songs had bewitched her heart ever since she was a child. Christmas carols always took her back to her earliest Christmases. Two tipsy hospital janitors stopped by their room and said that they wanted to sing two Christmas carols to the couple and the newborn child. Their first carol was *Joy to the World*. Then, they asked Mama Shenice if she had any requests for another carol before they moved on up the hallway.

A minute or two after the janitors had finished singing their next carol- *O Little Town of Bethlehem*, who was to walk into the room but L.C. Greenwood, Dwight White, and Mean Joe Green of the Pittsburgh Steelers vaunted Steel Curtain Defense. Man! Back in the day those three men made a wall of steel so thick that no train could plow through it without getting mangled out of shape. I mean these three men were stronger than any three men together in the world that you could imagine. These three men were a world of physical and also financial difference from the singing janitors. They were huge. Not only were they monsters physically, each about the size of a camel or an ox, they were all three very well dressed brothers. They had enough bling on them to blind you for a moment if you weren't careful. They even had that special cologne smell that you can smell every once in awhile on a rich brother. These three football stars looked so rich that they probably wouldn't bother to stoop down and pick up a priceless pearl if one was lying at their feet.

JL was stunned when he saw them. He immediately knew who they were. Shenice had no idea who these intruders were that were bothering her. As far as she was concerned they were just faces interrupting her need to rest. JL really wanted to ask them for some autographs while Shenice only wanted some privacy. The three Steelers apologized for interrupting. They said that they'd just happened to be walking through the maternity ward doing some charity visitation. They had been told that a new baby had been born and they wanted to pay their respects to the parents.

Pittsburgh Jesus

Each of them held the sleeping little Jesus in their hands with care for a moment. They each smiled at the baby and each of them bounced him ever so gently. When Mean Joe Green held baby Jesus he smiled and whispered "how innocent!" When JL heard this he thought of Mean Joe's Coke commercial and couldn't help but to laugh quietly to himself. It wasn't how JL ever imagined that these three Steel Curtain legends would ever behave in a thousand years of Sundays.

It seemed like a lifetime to JL. Actually, the three Steelers only stopped by for two or three minutes at the most. Before they left, however, they gave mother and child a golden Steelers Terrible Towel, some nice flower fragranced baby-wipes, and a nice silver black-and- gold Steeler logo keychain as little Christmas gifts.

JL kept that keychain and that terrible towel for the rest of his life. He passed the keychain on to Jesus when he was dying on his deathbed. JL never did drum up the courage to ask these three gods for their autographs-somehow it didn't seem the right time or place. He also realized that another time and place would probably never come his way again. That's life.

Not many newborns get visitors like that when they're in the hospital, and all of this just convinced JL how special their little baby would become. Maybe their boy would one day become a famous football or basketball player and he could tell people interviewing him that he'd meant Mean Joe Green at the moment when Jesus was born. JL hoped that at least his boy would go to school and get a decent job and maybe find a nice girl and give him some grandkids even if the baby never became famous or anything like that. All JL knew was that it was pretty cool that three great Steelers would take the time out of their busy holidays in the middle of the season with just a few days before their playoff game with Don Shula and the Miami Dolphins. They could've been home with their families; yet here they were, doing some charity visitation on Christmas and paying their respects to a new little family.

As the three Steelers were walking out of the room another baby doctor, Dr. Balakian, came to check on the boy. The doctor said out loud with wonder:"*Lord in Heaven! Let me depart in peace! I thought I'd seen everything but I just saw the three best defensemen in the NFL in this room! Did you get their autographs?*" JL smiled and mournfully whispered, "No."

Chapter Three:
Childhood

1. Papa

What else could be said about JL? The man was an honest maitre'de. He was as clean as an old Irish Catholic priest marooned on a deserted island filled with snakes. JL was as good a man as you'd ever meet. You could trust both your soul and your pocketbook with him.

While everyone else in his family was living their lives to the beat of Earth, Wind, and Fire, and Kool and the Gang, and James Brown all blaring loudly at once - JL was listening to Coltrane and Miles Davis on the loop going on inside his head. JL was a man of measure, and no more so than when everyone else was rocketing out of control like some spaceship trying to reenter the earth's atmosphere at a zillion miles a second. The man was as solid as an old oak in the forest. He was as silky in his style as a fine French lady's linen nightgown falling to a candle-lit bedroom floor.

There was nothing special about the man. His only claim to fame was that he'd had once heard El-Hajj Malik al-Shabazz, Malcolm X., preaching in Harlem. It was at a rally about a year before Malcolm was gunned down at the Apollo Ballroom. The way JL told it, he'd actually met X. In actual fact, he was just a big admirer. If the Stargell-naming idea didn't catch on with Shenice - JL also had ideas about naming the boy Malcolm X. Scott. JL kept a picture of both Malcolm and Martin together taped up on his bedroom wall. Mama Shenice showed it to me once and said that it was the only time that the two men ever actually met in person. JL had lived through all the drama in the 60's and had his opinions about it all. Mostly, however, JL was just going through life trying to get by and make ends meet. He didn't have any time to be a philosopher or poet about all that was wrong with the world. He was too busy working to figure all that stuff out.

JL didn't travel much. That was one thing, however, that he wanted to do if he ever won the lottery. JL had visited Philadelphia and had seen the White House and the Capitol in Washington D.C. when he was a little kid. The farthest travelling he'd ever done was to visit Expo '67 in Montreal, Quebec with his father who was then too old to drive. His pops offered to pay for the 16-year old JL's expenses if he'd do the driving for him. That was a great trip. Most of the folks up in Quebec didn't even speak English. Folks were drinking wine at all hours of the day and didn't seem to have much time for the black-white prejudices that were everyday life back home in the States. JL also liked it when he saw that some farmers were selling long loaves of homemade French bread along the side of the road in little brick ovens. Try eating that bread with some strawberry jelly or with some cheese! The food on that trip was delicious. Most of all, JL felt it was nice to spend some relaxing time with his pops.

One of the things that JL loved most was to talk about was the Scott family. He loved the stories of Mama Rebecca Simpson from Bedford and Papa John Paul – JP - Scott. None of his ancestors were royalty but, to him, they were all the same as kings. JL's grandfather, JP, was the first African-American principal to work in Harrisburg. He was a strict disciplinarian who taught Latin and Greek. Grandpa was also a big community man, a respected 33rd degree Mason in the Most Worshipful Prince Hall Grand Lodge of Free and Accepted Masons Chosen Friends Chapter #43 over on Hanover Street. Grandpa was following in the footsteps of his own father, the honorable John P. Scott who served as Grand Master during World War I and helped to lay the cornerstone at the Wesley Union A.M.E. Zion when it was over on Forster Street. This group was very proud that one of their first members was none other than the Reverend Absalom Jones when they were still the African Lodge over in Philly. Professor Scott also served as the superintendent of the local A.M.E. Zion Sunday school for 48 years which he always said was 47 years too much.

JL worked hard all of his life. The bills never stopped so he had no choice. JL never took a day of welfare and, even when sick, he showed up for work. His only regret was that he never felt like he had enough time to be with family. The hours were long. JL usually had to work on weekends and holidays. Even with all of the hours he pulled, he barely made it from paycheck to paycheck. Even though JL was laid off many times he always saved a little to see his family through. He'd often have to bite his lip when some new boss would question him about how many different jobs he'd already had, and especially when they wondered out loud if it was because he was lazy or irresponsible.

One thing about JL- he was very proud to be a waiter and that explains a lot about who he was. Service is a difficult task but it's what he relished. JL was a man of precise detail. The crystal always sparkled. The silverware always shone. The linens were folded to perfection. His eye was on each and every millimeter of the table. JL would go through an evening dinner engagement the same way that a brain surgeon would precede through an operation with the greatest of attention to the smallest detail.

Because of JL's job, Mama Shenice and Jesus knew about all kinds of food. JL would bring home Wellington Beef and Maryland crabs and cherrystone clams. Mama Shenice loved it when her man would bring home some leftover steamship roast beef. When the tips were good on a given day JL would let Jesus count his change. Jesus was amazed as a little boy how many fifty cent pieces his Pop had. Pop probably had bag-fulls of gold. That's where Jesus learned to do numbers like a wizard. Jesus remembered that his pops also always used to tip using two-dollar bills since he said that it was not only special, but it was twice as much as a one dollar note!

Very simply, JL always tried to do the right thing. After Shenice had baby Jesus she went back to Auntie Marion's for about a month. When JL took Shenice and the baby back to the hospital for their one month checkup and vaccinations, he also took the day off and the three of them went to the Justice of the Peace office in Pittsburgh. Instead of a honeymoon, JL and Shenice went to the Pittsburgh Hilton at Point State Park. They enjoyed a fancy vanilla ice-cream sundae with nuts and hot fudge sauce as their way to celebrate. They were so happy and that was all that really mattered to both of them. They had a new life. Now they were legally married. That weekend, Shenice and the baby moved in with JL into his tiny apartment up on Bennet Street in Homewood-Brushton. They were all finally able to live together under one roof: Good times.

JL became the guardian of his adopted son. He was the best friend to his wife Shenice Richardson, the only love of his life. Granted, when she first told him, back in Harrisburg, that she was going to have a baby it was a major speed bump because babies aren't exactly the sexiest things in the world. All of JL's friends at work had told him to forget about her and just go to the club, get drunk, bang some stranger to get her off of his mind, and then have nothing to do with her or her kid ever again.

That was not his style. He once did seriously considered breaking off their engagement. That was right after he proposed at Thanksgiving when he began to think about how tied down he was gonna be as the father of this kid that wasn't even his own. His friend LaVar encouraged him: he told JL just to get out of town without calling or leaving a note. LaVar said he should just go out to California or Tampa and start over without all of the baggage of having to take care of a new mother and child. When JL thought about this, he realized that all he really wanted to do was spend time with Mama Shenice. Even though he wasn't the papa (and didn't know who was), it only seemed right to be there for her when she needed him the most.

Even still, trying to take care of a pregnant woman is one of the hardest jobs in the world. Men think they know women because they enter inside them and, in the case of Shenice and JL, because she would drink in his every word. But, a pregnant woman is way beyond a man's comprehension. They are as mysterious to a man as an E.T. alien would be to a class of terrified kindergarteners. There is something about a pregnancy that changes everything for a woman in a way that a man never could begin to understand. That little demanding chunk of jumping life growing inside them takes them far away from the ordinary.

JL never once flinched when folks questioned him marrying a woman who already had a baby. So many folks in this world act like wolves. JL always dismissed the haters who challenged Shenice's story about some mystical, celestial nighttime rape that'd brought her baby into the world. Whenever JL would struggle with these questions, he'd work them out while shining silverware or ironing linens or washing crystal. He'd never talk to anyone but God. Knowing things doesn't usually change things anyway. Understanding things is kinda like the consolation prize, the booby-prize, in our lives.

2. Answering a Dream

JL had been most proud of his work for the highly esteemed Hunt Valley Inn in Baltimore. He'd also worked at some of America's other finest restaurants and hotels, such as the Hotel Hershey, the Harrisburger Hotel, and the Penn Harris Hotel. Those were some fine establishments where the Governor, and other notables, such as Joe Lewis and Duke Ellington stayed when they were in town long before JL was around. But, JL did once serve Dick Nixon at the Hotel Hershey after he'd left the White House. President Nixon talked about how much he loved his family and left a nice tip.

JL had thought that he'd only be in Pittsburgh for a short time until he could take his wife and baby back to Harrisburg or to Baltimore. The first thing he needed was to save some money for a car. JL was a man who always dreamed. My grandmother used to say, a cat always dreams of mice and JL always dreamed of making life easier for his loved ones. If it is true that the purest hearts are those who dream the most, JL was a saint. He would lie down and dream for hours. He conversated with the legions of angels swirling inside of his head while he slept. As soon as his head hit the pillow his breathing would be as measured as a pacing night-watchman. It was in sleep that he worked out the struggles of the present and plans for the future. JL would also wake up from his dreams the hungriest he'd ever feel all day.

The night that Jesus was born, JL had a deeply troubling - but clear as day - dream that he'd eventually need to get his fiancée and baby back to Harrisburg. The dream told him that the boy wasn't safe in Pittsburgh. JL filed that thought away. He was a man who usually went with his gut instincts but, since his job was still going strong, he decided to stay put for awhile.

When Jesus was about two years old there was a race riot in Homewood-Brushton. The infant was almost killed when a bottle flew through the Scott's front window and crashed into the crib where Jesus usually slept. This reminded JL of his dream from two years before. This time, he acted quickly. Since there were all kinds of craziness going on, the feeling that he'd had in his dream came back again. JL made plans to go back to Harrisburg.

JL had saved a little money and was able to borrow a little more from his friend, LaVar Arrington. He bought an old 1974 Honda hoopdy that would probably just be able to get them back to Harrisburg if they were lucky. It was a long five hours drive. If you've ever travelled with a two-year old on the expressway for a few hours, crying all the time while you are trying to avoid the trucks, you know what I mean. You also know why they call kids at that age, the "terrible two's."

3. The Pentecost of Mrs. Shenice Catherine Richardson-Scott

Nobody gets a better gift than the gift of a good mama. Sometimes, however, a tired-out mother finds that she herself has nowhere to turn but to the Lord Jesus Christ for relief from all of the stress in life. Women inspire other women. When a girl becomes a mama something snaps inside and that may be why so many women turn to the Holy Bible and to the Lord Jesus Christ from all of that dancing and partying and all of those fickle, immature, men-friends once they've had their first baby.

Whatever it was, when young Shenice became Mama Shenice, she began to read the Holy Bible like it was nobody's business. The holy book seemed to become attached to her. It never left her sight. She underlined every verse in red. She became an intense prayer warrior on her knees. She'd walk around her room singing in tongues - the fiery prayer-language of the Holy Ghost - to her newborn child. She'd wake the birds up at dawn with her shouting to the sky above. Mama Shenice would talk to God Almighty by the hour the same way that un-marrieds would talk on the phone by the hour to their boyfriends. Mama believed in the gift of Holy Ghost fire with the evidence of speaking in tongues. You'd hear her by the hour shouting out words only heaven could understand that came from deep within her soul: *"A la sham balla allah sham om shalla so kre goog kaa gai! A la sham ham ballah am sha halah sobre ocho sag ga kai! Kon digi ha wa! Kon digi ha wa! Kon digi ha wa! Hallelujah!"*

Mama Shenice slept with the Holy Bible in her bed. She especially loved the book of Revelations with all of the foretelling of the "End of Time" and she studied pamphlets and listened to radio programs about the signs of the end times and the coming deeds of the last-days antichrist.

As she read the powerful word of God, things started to become clearer and clearer to her. Mama Shenice was now certain that the fig tree had borne forth its blossoms. One day, a white sister named Marge Cramer, told her that the end-time vials in heaven were about to be poured out. The river Euphrates would soon enough become the dry creek bed that was foretold by the heavenly angels to the seven churches. The four horsemen had already loosed their four steeds from their four eternal barnyards. The final, end-time desolation of the temple was about to happen: Any day now. One generation would not pass away till all these things would be fulfilled. The fig tree had already borne fruit and set forth its blossoms. Now was the season to prepare to meet the bridegroom. Mama Shenice determined to join the watchtower saints so that one day she'd stand among the 144,000 witnesses dressed in white garments on the final day of all eternal glories.

She learned all about the end times from the Pastor C. J. Oliver, pastor of the Bethel Baptist Church. Basically, along with the nine apostolic gifts of the Holy Ghost and the baptism of fire, that was all that Brother Oliver preached about. This living church was a godsend for the new Mama. Shenice felt like she'd finally found her place and her people. It was at Bethel Baptist that she discovered a harbor in a cold world that didn't understand her pains. It was at Bethel Baptist that she literally met the Risen Christ in a divine revelation while praying. Master, King, Christ Jesus, the eternal Lord and crucified Son of God Almighty appeared in glowing ordainments of heavenly lights just to her in person. Mama fell to the ground in a trance and was slain in the Spirit just like Saul was thrown down from his donkey on the Damascus Interstate.

Bethel Baptist, and Pastor Oliver, showed Mama Shenice the handle to the doorway of her life. She'd been looking for this a long time. It took a lot of work to raise a crying baby and now Mama no longer did it all alone. She now lived with the help of the fire of the Holy Ghost and with the prayer language and with all of the nine apostolic gifts. It was no longer her that lived but it was Christ who now lived through her. She was just a vessel fit for the Master's use. Mama Shenice had Holy Ghost power flowing like electricity through her for the first time in her life. She was burning up like Joan of Arc did in all of those movies she saw as a kid. Of course, she'd been a Christian all her life. She'd asked the Lord Jesus Christ into her heart to be her personal Lord and Savior at the altar one Sunday morning when she was seven years old. But now, she knew the mighty power of Pentecost. Now, she'd become slain with the power of the Holy Ghost. She was cleansed, purified, and baptized with both fire and water with all of the nine divine evidences. The soft waves of Shekinah from God Almighty had come down on Mama like the waves of a warm soaking hot tub Jacuzzi filled with flowers.

Mama Shenice now had a holy fire burning white-hot inside of her. She loved her sweet Christ the Lord Jesus with all of her heart. Prayer felt like the secure pathway of travelers lost in the snowy mountains or like how a sailor threatened with shipwreck felt when they came to solid ground. If a man held onto both his daughter and wife after a shipwreck he might have to let one of them go to survive but Jesus would never let you drown in the tempest. No more would Mama trust in the arm of flesh that faileth.

After Pentecost came to Mama, she stopped cleaning houses and spent every day with her baby down at the Bethel Baptist Church in Coverdale. Aunt Marion and Uncle Sam went to this Pentecostal house of miracles on Sundays and Wednesdays. Mama Shenice, however, asked Pastor Oliver if she could go every day and anoint the seats with anointing oil and pray over the place so the Holy Ghost of God would fill it up with His power, fire, and love and that all of the demon spirits from hell's flames would be cast into outer darkness. Pastor Oliver could recognize a handmaiden intercessor when he saw one. He gave her the keys and it wasn't long before a deep cleansing, miracle, healing, revival of fire broke out in Bethel Baptist the likes of which no one had seen since the great cleansing revival work of 1971. The folks at Bethel Baptist were good folks and they thanked God for Mama Shenice. They prophesied that Mama was a prophetess sent from God Almighty and that her son had a call of the Eternal God on his life to shake the nations from his beginnings among them in South Pittsburgh.

Being with Pentecostal believers more and more, and less with worldly doubters had other benefits. True saints didn't doubt her miracle story about the African angel. They encouraged Mama to go on into her high calling of prevailing faith and visionary prayer. She liked the saints at Bethel Baptist because they didn't harbor uncertainties like a neglected kitchen harbors rats and mice. There wasn't a liberal bone in their bodies. These saints knew who God Almighty was and who the resurrected Lord Jesus Christ was, and that He was the only way to heaven and all of them were filled with the fire of the Holy Ghost with the evidence of speaking in the heavenly language of love. The Lord Jesus Christ was the only way, the only truth, and the only life, and no man could cometh unto the father up above in the sky except through the J-man. Hairy Krishna, Buddha, or Chairman Mao couldn't save nobody.

While those Pentecostal saints could not doubt her fire for the Holy Ghost, I bet that they never once imagined – even for a second - that Mama Shenice had been a prostitute or was an insane lady. The saints at Bethel Baptist also would give Mama a five or a ten dollar bill on some Sundays, or help her with her laundry, or, with watching the baby, so that she could have a few hours of soaking, intercessory prayer in the deep repast of holy dreams and heavenly visions.

The miracles and the fire-revival lasted for the first nine months of 1980. Then, just as the Steeler season was beginning; first the faith of the brothers, and then, also of the sisters, began to flag noticeably. Pastor Oliver was the first to discern this spiritual change. He said that God

Almighty was moving on from them because folks had stopped coming out for prayer and giving their tithe. God was about to write "Ichabod" over their doorposts. The cares of the world hath blinded them: "Thou hast sold thy birthright for a mess of pottage." Some of the saints had stopped waiting for the angel with the crown of gold on his head with the sharp sickle in his hand with the loud voice. Some of the saints had just decided to watch Steeler football on Sunday instead of laboring in the travails of intercessory prayer. When Bradshaw got injured, Pastor Oliver said the city was cursed for their sins. The services got shorter so that folks could get home by 1 P.M. Even the seven heavenly cherubim who had charge of the holy fire in the heavenly vials and who gathered the cluster of grapes also seemed to have thrown these into the great winepress of God Almighty's wrath. God's Judgment was about to fall and woe to all.

Other saints, like JL, may've become backsliders, but Mama Shenice never fell away. Once the attendance started to drop, so did the miracles of fire and the words of prophecy. There were no more visions of wheatfields or ocean waves telling of God's plans. There was a famine in the land of Beth-el. Finally, Shenice also stopped going to church every day. In October of 1980, Mama and JL moved in to his apartment in Homewood-Brushton. Being poor and a new mother without daily revelations meant that now she went into a kind of auto-pilot. The baby was walking and there was less hours in the day for prayer. The terrible-twos were the final straw in Mama's anointed season of Holy Ghost revival.

From 1980 onwards, Mama Shenice mostly stayed at home under the watch-care of JL. Mama never was one of those ladies who spent time decorating rooms with plastic flowers or tree branches from craft stores. Who had the extra money for that? Mama became a visitor again, even in her own home. After Bethel Baptist, she never really tried to make any friends of her own until after her son started bringing his friends around the house. On some Sunday mornings, instead of going to churches brimming with backsliders, sometimes she'd just stay home and watch the Rev. Dr. Oral Roberts, Richard, and the Worldly Action Singers and pray with them in the holy language of heaven.

I've already said a lot about Mama Shenice. I have to tell you, however, that she's so much of the story for me about Jesus. I don't know how it all works together, but the fact is that she's still here while he has gone on. In that way, she's some kind of connection for me. I miss her when she's not around, and I feel good when Mama is close. Whenever I meet Mama – even after all that has gone on in these last few years – I feel like I've just spent a calm afternoon at a warm, relaxing beach. One of Mama's hugs is as good as a soft, cool ocean breeze coming off the Gulf of Mexico.

Mama is still something of a loner; mostly quiet and shy, but she'll always talk to anyone who wants to reflect on the seven bowls of the revelations, or the mighty miracles of King Jesus. She still calls out to God Almighty on long and lonely nights. Mama is anchored in the blessed peace of the Eternal God. Maybe, that's why she was such a rock to JL, and to her baby Jesus, and, to all of us who knew her. She always told all of us to keep close to God Almighty. Mama gave that way of thinking to her son. Shenice Richardson always had a different way of looking at things.

I think about Mama Shenice all the time; even though I rarely see her anymore. Did I tell you how much she loved flowers? Mama knew the Latin names of the flowers and could tell you a story about any flower like they all were her adopted babies. She was full of surprises. Mama loved perfume and always burned candles in her rooms whenever she was at home. She always had a song on her lips. You would've thought, because she was so beautiful, that she would've had more kids; but she never did. This was especially strange since JL had always wanted a child together with her.

Even though Mama's hands were soft, and as slender as could be, for an aspiring pianist, most of her life led to wrinkles and aching, arthritic pains. Life was hard for that woman in so many ways. I remember her crying out to God Almighty in her intercessions for a miracle-touch while she waived her Evangelist Oral Roberts miracle prayer-cloth up in the air to reach the heavens. I remember her wailing tears whenever I hear a sad or soulful song, like Otis Redding's "dock of the bay," on the car radio.

Most of all, Shenice Richardson was a mama. Nobody cooked a sweet potato pie like Mama could. She had the right combination of cinnamon and nutmeg and she liked to put some yams in it instead of just sweet potatoes. Mama made it taste just like candy yams in a pie plate. Mama always made sure that her son was well-dressed even if the clothes had to come from the Salvation Army Thrift Store or, whenever she came into a bit of money, from the discount racks at K-Mart.

Even though the world is brimming with billions of folks, all that mattered to her was her precious and only son, Jesus. Being a mama was her life. Everything she did was toward keeping her boy safe, warm, and fed. In the end, however, she wasn't able to protect him from killing hatred. Mama couldn't save him from his friends who drained the life out of him with their neediness. Like so many other Mamas, she gave, and gave, and gave, until there was nothing left to give. Mama Shenice cooked, sewed, and cleaned for others, but no one ever really took care of her.

4. Harrisburg

Pittsburgh Jesus grew up in Harrisburg. He became strong, tall, and smart enough. The capitol city of the state of Pennsylvania is out of the way from the other, bigger Eastern cities. I guess you actually can get there from Philly or New York, but I'm not sure if you need to switch trains or buses to get there. It's really more like a little town that is auditioning to become a big city. It was a great place, however, to raise a family compared to more dangerous places like Washington or Baltimore.

The Scott's lived in an apartment at the corner of Fulton and Rieley Street about four blocks from the river. The apartment was like a cave and took up the entire ground floor. It had seven rooms and was spacious. A fake stairway ran up to the second floor that stopped at a wall. No one ever seemed to know if there was anything behind the wall, but the stairway was a fun place to play games on. You could pretend that each step was like a ladder that was going somewhere important.

JL and Shenice didn't have many visitors at their apartment in Harrisburg. Not even many of their family members came by very often. That was okay for JL and Shenice. They kept pretty much to themselves and had their own lives where Jesus was the center. Whenever JL had a little time off work – and that wasn't all that much – he'd use it to fix up the house a little bit more. Step by step, he was turning this apartment into a home with his own signature. At first, JL put plastic over the windows, but later, he saved to buy some nice storm windows so the house wasn't too drafty in the winter. The man was always busy with his hands trying to make things better and to make life easier.

As the years went on, the apartment became a beehive of games and activity. Once school let out somebody was running in and out of that place any time of the day. One summer, Jesus built a fort up on the roof where his friends would get bottle-caps from Wolf's grocery store and shoot at the other kids in the 'hood. Mama worked on making the apartment more of a home with some art that she was always looking for. She put up a few prints of the Harrisburg Capitol and some landscape scenes that she bought from a guy who used to come around the 'hood trying to sell driftwood.

Harrisburg was a decent place for a black boy to grow up because it was small, and slow enough, so that a person could learn enough; but not too much. It was the only place, anyway, where JL knew to take his bride and baby away from any drama. Even though he liked Pittsburgh and the pay was good, he decided to get back home; where he knew everybody. Now, he had a wife and a boy to worry about. JL thought that there'd be less worry in Harrisburg and it was no problem for him to get his old job back. Before you knew it, his work kept getting better and better.

It was probably a good move to leave the 'Burgh in terms of what was best for his family. He still kept up a little bit with LaVar and some of the other folks that he'd worked with in the 'Burgh. One of neighbors, Mrs. Narves Gammage lost one of his sons, around aged 30 years, after they moved. Johnny G. was stopped "for driving erratically" by Sergeant Keith Hendy down on Route 51 at about 2AM in some redneck town called Brentwood. At the time, Johnny was in a borrowed black Jaguar that belonged to his cousin Ray Seals, the football player from Syracuse. Seven minutes after he was stopped, Johnny G. was stone-cold dead. Four cops from Baldwin-Whitehall used their flashlights to sink Johnnie's head three feet into the pavement of that damned street. Then they choked him and stepped on his head. The last thing the Sergeant heard him say was: "I'm only 31, Keith."

It made national news. The NAACP went ballistic when Sergeant Hendy got off scot-free and the other three only got involuntary manslaughter from Allegheny County and never served time. In fact, the main feisty cop, John Vojt even got a promotion! Later, it came out that this cop also probably killed one of his ex-girlfriends although all of that also was swept under the rug. The only juror who voted for a conviction of the cops who killed Johnny G. was also the only black juror. When they had a retrial, the whites who ran Allegheny County made sure that all of the jurors were white: Surprise! Surprise! Soon enough, however, everyone had forgotten about it. Everyone has also forgotten all about Michael Ellerbe or Charles Dixon over in Mount Oliver. JL felt so hurt for Mama Narves and JL never forgot about that boy; poor Johnny G.

When I think about the life of Jesus I think about drama and dazzle and not about patience and boredom. Most of his life, just like most of this world, is full of uneven fullness. He had a wonderful childhood and played up a storm. Later in his life, he'd be known for miracles, teachings, a dramatic death, and a strange conclusion. Early on, however, Jesus was just one poor black kid among many; it would not be easy to find him in even the smallest crowd. A big day for the boy would be when his Papa would take him for a Vanilla Malted Milk Shake at the Shake Shop at Sixth and

Pittsburgh Jesus

Muench. JL would get paid every other Thursday. After all the bills were paid, the Scott's would go to the Shake Shop for hamburgers and one order of French fries to be shared around.

For most of his life there was not much special about Jesus. For those years that he lived in Harrisburg, every day was pretty much like the day before. The family house was nothing to speak of. His family would not get into any newspaper or gain any notoriety. Most of life happens in places like Harrisburg where all that happens is that a lazy river goes through a valley. Babies grow up to be kids; kids grow up to be adolescents; then kids go through puberty; then they become young men and women. They have kids of their own and the cycle starts all over again. What changes are the names and not much else: Mediocre frozen-pizza living delivered cheaply in a cardboard box. The childhood of Jesus was about the same things as mine: girls, sports, movies, pizza, and being poor. He became good friends with the mediocre and the insignificant commonplace. What else is there to say about the obscure years of the stay-at-home Jesus?

The biggest single, regular event of his life happened when his Papa would take Jesus to watch the opening game of the Harrisburg Senators minor-league baseball team and when Mama would take him every year to watch the fireworks alongside the river. JL used to tell stories about the old Negro leagues and especially about Satchel Paige, Cool Papa Bell, and Josh Gibson, who he half-reverently called *the Trinity*. He said that Josh Gibson of the Homestead Grays was much better than Babe Ruth. He told how old Satchel Paige of the Kansas City Monarchs once sent his entire outfielders in and then struck out the side to prove to everyone that they had no chance against him. The way he told it, Jackie Robinson got booed so loud you couldn't hear yourself think when he first came up to the big leagues with the Brooklyn Dodgers. Those white fans would still be booing him even now, if it wasn't for the fact that Pee Wee Reese came up to Jackie, put his arm around him before the start of that first game. Those must've been tough times for blacks in baseball. These stories, as well as long afternoons and conversations with his dad, are why he was one of the few people I knew who actually cared anything about baseball. JL wanted to give his son a love of baseball and, although the boy never played the game, he certainly enjoyed relaxing at the ballpark for an afternoon or evening with a few friends, a few hotdogs, and a few beers whenever he got the chance.

Whenever both of his parents were working Jesus would stay at home with other relatives and, as he got older, more and more time was spent with his grandparents. It seems that over the years they softened a little bit although they never really talked to Shenice about how they treated her when she was a 16 year-old dropout. Anyway, the grandparents now loved Jesus as if he was their own. They dreamed for him big dreams as they'd once dreamed for his Mama. Jesus listened to all of the advice that they gave him. He did his chores and helped out neighbors if they needed something. He was a good boy - an intelligent kid, and he often lost himself in the pages of a book after school. He'd read anything he could get his hands on. The librarian at school kept feeding him a steady diet of biographies and history stories of American wars gone by. Maybe the librarian gave him that stuff because she liked those books herself, or maybe there was some other reason, but the bottom line was that Jesus could tell you more about what happened to the soldiers on the last day of the Alamo or to the Indians at the Battle of Little Big Horn and Custer's Last Stand than you thought anybody would ever be able to know.

5. Baptism

Jesus Scott was baptized when he was 12 years old just like everybody else in his neighborhood. He was baptized in the old Wesley A.M.E. Zion Church down on Fifth and Camp by his uncle, old Pastor Ron the Baptizer. That preacher lived for those baptism services: It was his best chance to shout about how folks were sinning and needed to turn away from their evils: He stirred the crowd. Christians needed to be more radical and old Wesley Zion was not yet as radical as it could get with Pastor Ron. Folks needed a baptism of unquenchable fire! The world was full of reprobates who were becoming more brazen as every evil day went by. That was why the saints of a holy and righteous God needed to be purified from *sensual appetites.*

Wesley Zion Church had baptism services once every summer on the steep banks of the Susquehanna River. The weather the day that Jesus was baptized was scalding hot. The heat was burning up the sidewalks while the water in the river was as cold as ice. What Jesus told me was how cold the water was and how a smog cloud brooded over the city that day. He said the Air Pollution Index on that day was through the roof. After Jesus was baptized, Pastor Ron shouted out for no known reason: *"It's him! It really is him! God Almighty is well pleased with you son! Mighty well pleased boy!"*

Wesley Zion was a church that worshipped the Eternal God of the normal, the common, and ordinary. Pastor Ron wore strange clothes- mostly purple and pink suits. He looked like a caricature of a player. You'd think he was out there trying to hustle his own mother or his little sister on the streets the way he would dress but Pastor Ron really didn't seem to care how he looked. You'd see him walking up and down Market and Thirteenth up on the hill in Harrisburg, passing out flyers about some upcoming church services. Most of the time he'd hang out and try to talk to brothers and sisters coming and going from the State Liquor Store and from Charles Wallace's barbershop. That old African was darker than the darkest black olive. He looked like a circus clown on the make in his mixed-up multicolored threads.

Pastor Ron pretty much lived off of corn bread and catfish for breakfast, lunch, and dinner. He was born and bred in the country, someplace called Owings Mills, Milford Mills, or someplace like that. It was one of those quiet villages with houses on top of hills where folks learn to love the moods of nature that most of us have never even noticed. Later, the pastor moved to the Randallstown area of Baltimore and got into some trouble as a young man. Even though most of that area was single family homes, Ron spent most of his time down in Walbrook Junction West Side with a gang he joined from the East Side. It wasn't all that long before he was forced to spend time in a Randallstown juvenile facility.

If you go into Baltimore Greenmount, Loch Raven, over by Morgan State, Edmonson Village, and Walbrook Junction, some folks are still telling stories about the crazy things Pastor Ron did before he became a pastor. He never told anyone about this part of his life because, as he said, *"it was all under the blood;"* whatever that meant. Some folks claim he killed an East Side man from Towson down in Greenmount just because the stranger looked like he might have some money on him.

Pastor Ron? The man got right up in your grill. Was he grumpy because he was unhappy with his own life? Was that why he tried to make everyone else miserable? One thing is sure Pastor Ron had more unfulfilled hopes than the inside of a Florida moving van had nicks and scratches.

Pastor Ron claimed he was called by the Almighty to be a voice; and not just an echo. Whenever he preached, it seemed like he was laughing, crying, and hyperventilating all at once. He made music on six or seven different scales all at once with his voice. Pastor Ron was not afraid to confront the saints for all kinds of vices that most other preachers simply overlooked. He often attacked Harrisburg's long-standing mayor for his deceptive practices and manipulative ways. The man ran the city like it was his own kingdom and had both the Democrats and the Republicans in his back pocket but he didn't scare Pastor Ron who called the mayor out for his private gallivanting with his posse of boy-toys: *"Mayor —you and your brood of vipers named this town after an Indian killer John Harris and you' all will one day stand before Almighty God!"*

Pastor Ron frequently called out one of the young ladies in the church, the daughter of Deacon Ridgeway, who had some kind of a drug problem. That turned out to be a big mistake. It seemed like he was trying to make enemies. After a few services some of the saints would go out of their way not to talk to him. A lot of the saints didn't like the man, and even more learned not to like him over time. None of that seemed to bother Pastor Ron. He definitely would've never won a popularity contest. He even criticized some of his deacons, especially Melvin "Toby" Massey and Elijah Watlington, for being members of the Masonic Prince Hall Lodge up at Fourteenth and Hanover even though they were some of the most respected pillars; and certainly the most generous financial contributors; in the congregation. He warned that the Masons walked secret paths that were crooked. Their secret worship to the false god called "JahBaLon" would one day come out into the open light.

The congregation at Wesley Zion was a wonderful collection of good, honest folks; most of the members were white- collar workers who got up every day and did what they had to do for the sake of their families. The church had a bunch of school-teachers, a couple of insurance agents, several aspiring entrepreneurs, Miss Annabelle Baltimore, three or four policemen, and a few secretaries who worked for the Federal Government over in some big offices in Mechanicsburg. For some reason, the undertakers in Harrisburg's black community seemed to mostly to go to Capital Presbyterian.

Pastor Ron didn't have a lisp like some preachers do, but he was still almost impossible to understand half the time. Mama Shenice liked it best when he'd talk about the thousand year reign of God and the first angel holding a great chain with keys to the abyss. Folks needed to heed the third angel and not to drink the wrath of an Eternal God's burning sulfur. One day the third angel would wear a golden sash and watch the sea turn to blood red.

In one sermon, Mama Shenice said that Pastor Ron shouted out that the Almighty and Holy God of the Wheels within the Wheels had impregnated some in his congregation with the Spirit of sunlight and all kinds of other strange statements. The saints barely even said Amen but God was coming soon to change all that. The Almighty was gonna move and the Eternal was gonna sweep away the anti-Christ forces of evil. The

Judge was gonna shake things up and make changes. The King of the Universe was not gonna sit back and be mocked, scorned, and slighted forever. It was the last days of the last days. Pastor Ron warned that the Holy Ghost was about to come down like a bulldog into their midst and chew at the ankles of all those hypocrites who had the mark of the beast or worshipped his vile image at an evil, secret altar in the basement of the JahBaLon loving, Masonic Prince Hall Lodge.

In another service Mama Shenice said that Pastor Ron once prophesied: *"The Word will rise. In fact, it is already rising in thy hearts, Akeem, Maurice, Derrick, Joyce, and Jarrett. I am not the word but I am the element. I am not bringing thee this Word but thou will not need to search for it either. Thou who art and thou who art to come, will behold the throne of the Beast set upon the seven hills. A tall Fisherman in thy river will catch red trout the size of skateboards and African elephants from thy zoo will run wild down thy streets. A white horse with a sword in his mouth will fall from the top of the Statue of Liberty and a necklace of gold will appear in every child's Halloween basket. A dragon with ten horns and seven bleeding heads will have the ways of a spotted leopard but the feet of a bear and the mouth of a silver lion. His feet will be made of clay and his number will be the number of a man. Give that 666-slewfoot a fatal wound to his double head! Bow down and worship on the sea of glass before the Lamb that was slain! Follow Him where He leadeth. The spirit will pierce thine heart but will thou bruise the serpent's head? Will thou recognize the holy word of fire? Art thou ready for the holy word of fire?"*

Pastor Ron experienced the fire of divine Holy Ghost prophecy. He once foretold that a great man would soon be coming into the midst of their church. Some of the saints thought it might be one of the players for the New York Knicks who had a relative who lived in the town. Most of the saints just weren't too sure and didn't really care. If somebody famous ever did show up, nobody knew about it or maybe nobody never recognized whoever it was whenever they came if they did come like the prophet had foretold.

Most saints just took a "wait and see" attitude whenever the Pastor received one of his words of prophecy. God Eternal's ways and Pastor Ron's ways were inscrutable and beyond figuring. It seemed like the messenger of the Almighty spake in parables, mysteries, and deep sayings that needed a level of Holy Ghost fire that most saints just never reached out to find. Trying to believe in all of these things was just too much work for most folks; and sometimes the Pastor would announce that one of his prophecies had come true in the unseen heavenly realms. Anyway, God's ways are beyond most of us.

Nobody thought that Pastor Ron was crazy. That was one possibility that no one had ever considered even for a second. Folks realized that he was a mighty man of God marching to his own heavenly drummer. Even he claimed more to walk in the heavenlies than here on the tired clay of this old earth. The saints were pretty sure that he was a man of God because – at the end of the day – he had a heart of gold and helped anybody that needed it. Folks didn't really understand what he was saying but they hoped that, if they stayed close to him, that all of their sins would be forgiven. At least, they felt that Pastor Ron would bring them some good luck or keep trouble away from the door when he was around. He was good people.

Folks in the church worked hard and lived simple, decent lives for the most part. The saints had the usual problems – cheating on their spouses, drinking, drugs, going into debt, fights with friends and family. But, every once in awhile, some kind of explosion happened in the church and accusations flew like sharpened knives.

One time, Deacon Ridgeway's daughter accused Pastor Ron of trying to rub himself all up in her breasts. She first told her Daddy but before long other saints were fuming about what might've happened. Ridgeway, a former Marine, was outraged. He took out his service pistol and dealt with what Pastor Ron had been accused of in the only way he knew how: Bam bam bam - Three shots to the head. The pastor fell straight down right in the parsonage and the carpet turned as red as fire. He was as dead as a dead catfish floating down the river. Nobody thought that pastor had really molested the girl because he just wasn't that kind of person, and she wasn't exactly the pure Virgin Mary. Ridgeway went to prison for life.

Folks were in shock but – you know how these things are – people forget about stuff sooner or later and move on. After a few months of Deacon Kler Jones trying his best to take over the preaching duties until things could get sorted out - the Bishop stepped in and found the church a replacement for Pastor Ron. Some young buck from the seminary named the Reverend Dr. Marchant Jefferson took Pastor Ron's pulpit and things sure quieted down after that. No more shouting or prophesies and no more baptisms down at the riverfront. Sooner or later, some of the old saints decided to move on to greener pastures and get under the anointing of one of those preachers who brought the fire of the Holy Ghost and not just a little candle of the truth flickering as frail as could be imagined.

6. Where's Jesus?

The year after Pastor Ron was shot in the head, and when Jesus was around 13, the boy went missing one time and his parents were worried about him to tears. They had no idea what had become of the child.

Jesus was a boy of surprises: It all started when JL and Mama Shenice told everyone that they were going on a special trip and wouldn't be back for a few days. They finally had a few coins to rub together so they decided to do something that they'd always wanted to do which was visit Amish country. Their plan was to eat all day at a huge smorgasbord restaurant they had heard about in Lancaster. Everything would've been fine except at the end of the first day, they got a call at their hotel that their son had not come home from school that day.

They got in their car and sped back to Harrisburg as fast as they could. When they got home they found that everyone in the 'hood was already looking for him. Folks guessed that since he was something of a prankster, it was probably nothing. He was probably hiding somewhere so he could see everybody work up a sweat. His Pop thought that he might've been hiding in the house or up on the roof or something like that. After a while, they sent out one of the neighbors to look over by the walk-bridge at Italian Lake because Jesus would often go over there to do a little fishing and some thinking.

Someone else checked around the A & P Supermarket because one of his friends said that they often saw him over there running some kind of errand or something for one of the old folks on the block. Mr. Fletcher even said that what had happened was that he'd ridden his bike all the way out to the Three B's Ice Cream Shop in Linglelstown Front Street because of how he loved so much their ice cream; and it was so rare that he had any time to go and enjoy some of it.

Jesus was nowhere to be found. That turned out to be not surprising because what had actually happened was that Jesus had gone out of town for the day. While everyone thought he was lost, he had simply had gotten on one of the Harrisburg High buses that were leaving that morning for a day-long field trip to the Smithsonian and the Holocaust Memorial Museums down in Washington D.C. That was something like a three hour drive away.

It wasn't until late that night that the school bus returned from the D.C. field trip. During that entire time, JL fretted about what a bad guardian he had been and Mama Shenice prayed up a storm while she was looking for him everywhere. *"Perhaps he has already begun- has already left me"*- she fretted to JL.

JL had no idea what Mama was talking about but he called the Harrisburg City police and told them about their lost child. Around midnight, a policeman called their house. He left the message that Jesus was up at the high school in the parking lot and needed a ride home.

Sure enough, they found him having the time of his life talking with the John Harris principal, some teachers, and some of the kids twice his age almost- college kids- about what they had seen at the Holocaust museum and how such a thing could happen. *"You sure have a smart kid!"* one weathery old black teacher, Dr. Raymon Curtiss, who had led the field trip, enthused to JL. *"That kid should work in a museum or own one someday. He's like a museum guide in the making. It's like he's madly in love with history learning and as curious as a goat. Jesus! Wonderful kid!"*

That old professor looked like a six-foot bag of a tortoise; a withered old human being with tortoise like-eyes and a pointy nose that seemed to be giving directions like a one-way street sign. Old Curtiss struck no confidence in JL at all by the baggy way that he dressed and by the way every sentence wandered like a lame dog into a ditch. All the old man could do was talk about how the boy knew every fact about the Nazi Holocaust against the Jews and all about the Armenian Genocide done by the Turks. All Mama and Pop cared about was losing their son and being frazzled for the last few hours. Now, they learn that their beloved boy had been out of state for the last fifteen hours under the oversight of some rickety old wizard of a man who himself was probably as lost as a goose in a blizzard.

Mama and Pop had different ideas about how to deal with the situation. What's done is done JL thought. Mama Shenice, however, wasn't about to leave it at that. She wanted to keep her son contained and controlled, but she was beginning to realize that those days were forever behind her.

As soon as the three of them got into JL's car, Mama Shenice went into the boy with a bolt of burning lightning: *"Why have you done this to us? Should a mother be treated like this? What on earth were you thinking? Washington is hours away. You just can't get on a bus like that! We've been looking everywhere for you and we've been worried sick!"*

Mama scolded him for going to the museum without them knowing about it. She wiped a river of some pent-up tears from her eyes. His answer was simple: He had heard some kids were going to a museum and he loved going to museums more than anything else in the world. He hadn't been to a museum in over a year and so he went. He said he felt happy at museums and never once felt the need to worry about his parents. Jesus said that he didn't understand why they were so worried or why they were searching for him.

The boy was growing up fast. He was as smart as a tack in a bag of marshmallows. Sometimes that boy of hers was not her boy at all. Jesus was just simply beyond her motherly understanding. Anyway, because Mama loved him like the sun in the sky she always prayed for him and worried for him whenever he was out of her sight – which was most of the time these days. Most of what his mama wanted for Jesus is what most mama's secretly want for their boys; to stay forever young and under their protective wing and watchful eye.

Most mamas wouldn't mind if their kids stayed poor snails living in a shell if that is what it took to keep them from having horrible things happen to them. Was there any way to put their kids in a bottle and just wait for the storms of growing older to pass on by? Parents are most afraid of what they cannot foresee. Waiting for their kids to get through the swamp of all the decisions in life might be the hardest part of being a parent – unless you learn not to care too much. We can't foresee what will happen to anybody and maybe that's a good thing.

One thing JL and Shenice were sure about, though, was that the days of knowing where their boy was was over: the playground or the basketball court or the neighbor's house. Now, with curiosity meeting mobility, Jesus could be wandering anywhere. For Mama Shenice and JL they knew that their only kid would soon be running off for good and then they'd be left in an empty house filled with only memories of his laughter. Even Harrisburg no longer seemed so small and safe anymore.

Even though JL – an adopted father after all - took care of Jesus like he was his own son, it was JL's fate that his own life would be swallowed up into the dramatic twists and turns of the story of the man Jesus. Mostly because of Shenice, life had been full of surprises for the handsome young James Scott. Most of his life, however, had been wafted up to heaven as an offering in the same way that the hours of his energy always seemed to go toward helping the grand banquets of others while he himself ate the simplest of foods at the most common of tables. Even the constants in his life, Shenice and Jesus, never seemed to belong to him as if he'd always need to make payments for them down at the rental store of his life. They were beautiful flowers in a vase belonging to somebody else. Sometimes, this made him sad and alone but he didn't really know why he felt that way. JL obviously loved Jesus, but at the same time, he never really quite understood what was going on with his adopted son. Shenice had also always been a riddle to the man. Neither of them every really *belonged* to him.

7. Wilderness

There were plenty of temptations that Jesus faced at John Harris Harrisburg High. Life was just beginning for him. There were drugs, drinking, girls, and gangs like everywhere else. The ladies sure were interested in him because he always took time to dress well and make sure that his corn-rows were perfect. He got compliments from the girls for being sweet and considerate. He wasn't one of those tough street guys.

The fact that he was six foot four inches meant that he was able to make it as a pretty good outside shooting point guard on the basketball team. Basketball probably helped keep him out of trouble. The worst thing he had to face was dealing with the rich, white kids from suburban schools who would insult the Harrisburg players as *niggers* and *coons*. They also made fun of their older uniforms which, by comparison, were not nearly as nice as the teams from Mechanicsburg and Camp Hill.

Papa JL gradually got sick as a result of the pressures of trying to start his own business. He had always wanted to open his own catering company. He had a friend, L.C. Carr, a bakery chef at the hotel where they worked, who he planned to have as his partner. Carr had sold him on the idea but Carr had a gambling problem and pretty soon JL was stuck with a lot of debt and he had to go find Carr and get him out of after-hour clubs and gambling joints. Carr also drank so the whole investment-gone-bad wore JL down. Mama Shenice tried to get him to go back and just work at the hotels. JL, however, was stubborn. He always wanted Jesus to be somebody and to take over a family business so JL could retire. That was part of the reason he moved back to Harrisburg in the first place.

At the beginning of 1994, JL got sick. On May 13, 1994, JL died suddenly of a heart-attack. It was a shock when his soul went flying off into the sky. There was no time to make sense of it because it all happened so fast. Folks always assumed he'd be around and it seemed like the strangest thing in the world to not be able to stop by and see him or give him a call since he was like rainwater – you could always count on him. That's why, for the brothers and sisters who knew him, the clock on the world seemed to stop that day. Who knows? Maybe those who believed in reincarnation were right and his soul flew off into sunny Africa and entered into the life of some baby girl being born in Igboland or somewhere else that very same morning. JL was like a pillar or a lamppost on the street that anybody could lean on and no one really noticed that he had needs of his own. Everyone who knew him was devastated for some reason that they couldn't quite explain. On the other hand, news of his death never even got into the Harrisburg paper. Why should it? He'd never been a politician, or a preacher, or some famous entertainer. He was only a good father and a good husband and a good cook.

Mama Shenice couldn't say a word for what seemed like a few days. She couldn't imagine life without her rock. Jesus couldn't believe that his pop had been here one day and was gone the next. For some reason, Jesus even felt guilty somehow as if he'd, in some unexplainable way, had something to do with his pop's death. What was gonna happen now to the mother and son? To top everything off, a few months earlier, when he first began to feel sick and slow down, JL had cashed out all of his insurance to try and keep his catering business going. His idea was to figure out a way to sell it off to someone else but he never got around to that. From a money point of view, his millions of hours working for other people had added up to nothing in the end. Mama Shenice recalled what Pastor Ron preached: *"Life was like a fleeting morning vapor or mist that appeareth for a moment before it was gone forever."*

After pop died, Jesus never really did show any interest – let alone any skill – in keeping the catering business going. He was only fifteen. There were still a few events scheduled and JL's family and friends took care of these as best as they could instead of cancelling them. But, the handwriting was on the wall. Nobody was taking new orders because brothers and sisters wanted their events catered by folks who left all the worry out of their plans and JL's attention to detail was what was now missing.

For the next three years Jesus and Mama Shenice stayed in the big house by doing odd-jobs and by taking donations from family. In the summers, and on weekends, Jesus got a job working for the city in a parks clean-up program that they had for inner-city youth. In his senior year at John Harris, Jesus got a decent full-time, well-paying job at a restaurant because he was JL's boy. JL had also wisely set aside a tiny bit of money in the bank and Mama Shenice stretched that out as long as she could. Jesus did great in his high school classes. His high school years went fast without any problems. The only thing he ever did was play a big role - Sancho Panza - in a high school version of a musical called the "Man of LaMancha." Jesus never got into any trouble with any of his teachers – except one white professor who was teaching African-American literature and history. Jesus was angry by the teacher's seeming indifference to the subject that he'd been paid to teach.

When it came time to graduate, the students at John Harris began to talk about what they were going to do with the rest of their lives. Most kids were going to try and find some kind of job somewhere – anywhere. A few of the smarter kids were angling to get some kind of scholarship for college. Some kids were going to start out at community college. For Jesus, college had never really been an option. Why spend four more years in school trying to learn from folks who were offering their services to you for a fee when you could learn from real folks for free and they didn't sit around in classrooms and offices. Anyway, it seemed that all the folks that he knew who went to college only went to get out of college with a better job and that logic seemed all turned around to Jesus.

The recruiters for the army swarmed around Jesus like mosquitoes to a fly-swatter. The Army, Navy, and Marines always were up at John Harris High School trying to recruit the young men of the school into their uniforms and away from the streets – "for their own good." Be all that you can be and be it all for Uncle Sam and for your country. It was money in the bank; a sure bet. The military would set you up, train you, and take care of you for the rest of your life - if you didn't get killed overseas. The recruiters told the guys that the ladies loved the look of men in uniforms and they would work out a lot on weights and get a lot of exercises and end up looking like Bo Jackson. There were some service men in the family and all of them had done well for themselves. Jesus had given the idea some thought but he really had trouble imagining himself in a uniform. He really wasn't much of a "uniform-guy." Meanwhile, it seemed like half of the boys of John Harris took the bait of the signing bonus and the promise of the steady money and a chance to travel to distant countries.

Jesus sure could've used the money if he had signed up with Uncle Sam. Times were tight. It wasn't looking like it'd get easier any time soon for the family. Since the bills never stopped for his Mama, Jesus gave her most of his restaurant paycheck. He also started to work also a little bit as a window-washer with the Tyrone Schulte's dad's Acme Window Cleaning Company. He quit after about two weeks. Jesus did good work but just wasn't motivated. Anyway, he still had his restaurant gig.

About a year out of high school, Jesus, and some of his friends got the idea that it'd be cool for them to try to make their millions by forming a band. Maybe that is something everybody thinks about doing once in their life with a gang of their friends but these guys made it happen. They formed a throw-back old-school singing group called the Emperors. That was when the sound of Philadelphia was trying to make a comeback and was still vital. Jesus taught himself the bass and played a little. Milton Brown played keyboards and Tyrone Schulte played the drums. Pepsi Jackson was on guitar alongside Scott. Edgar Moore, Steve Stephens and Donald Brantley all sang.

They even made a record, called *Karate* that made a wave or two around Harrisburg. A dance was associated with it and most of the folks at Lawson's, the 612, and the Mella Ballou all knew the Karate: "*Get out your soul bag baby 'cause we got a new dance goin round. It's that dance called Karate. It's putting all the other dances down. Dig this dance. Karate is the hottest dance in town....* "

Things were going real well with the Emperors. Soon Milton and Jesus tried to open a club along with Bob Hubbard, their booking agent. They took over the *Raven* and renamed it *The Rope* because that allowed them to save money on the sign by turning the "*a*" into an "*o*" and adding the "*p*" and dropping the "*v*" and the "*n*." The idea was to have a club that catered to teenagers. But, there wasn't enough work and guys started to marry and take different jobs. You know how it goes. Music changes and people were settling down and some of them became tired giggin' on the weekends. Their manager, George Milton, ripped them off and before long; an ancient Carlos Santana even redid Karate as "Everybody's Everything."

The band evaporated and everyone moved on. After Jesus gave up his restaurant gig to try to work more on his music, he began to feel a big hurt in his wallet. Because the band wasn't making enough, and because he still wanted to help out his mama, Jesus decided to make some extra cash by selling some weed to friends. The money helped a little but he never had the drive to be a businessman.

One of the proofs that Jesus wasn't exactly cut out for business was that whenever he did have some free time, he often wasted hours of it by helping some white guys up at a homeless shelter kind of a place up at the top of a hill on 15th Street. It was run by the Brothers of the Catholic Worker House, Brother Ned Tonoyan and Brother Bruce Leonard Brown. They had a big black Virgin Mary outside their door. They'd always hang out banners out of their windows about how a merciful and loving God hated the death penalty or stealing from the poor or some other such announcement as if it were something for the evening news. Whatever. At least they were there and had something to say. Bruce was black as midnight, but Jesus wasn't quite sure that Brother Ned, a white guy, was really much of a brother.

On the other side of the coin, the guy never left. When Brother Bruce skipped town with some money from a big donation or something, Brother Ned just kept plugging away as oblivious as could be to how hard the whole thing really was to make some kind of difference on the streets. I'm sure you've all met these kinds of white-kid idealists who think they can change the world and all they really end up doing is growing old and being some kind of question mark to people as to what exactly they are trying to do or why they are trying to do it. How can you argue with a merciful and loving God anyway? If He wanted them there, then that was the end of it anyway, and so most people just left them alone. This place opened around '96 or '97 and that is where most people looked for Jesus when they were trying to find him. He'd hang out there and talk for hours to whomever else was hanging out there with him.

Mama Shenice had always been a devout religious lady to the most intense degree imaginable, but Jesus himself even began to go to church with her, listen to the sermons, and even read the Holy Bible every day. Maybe religion made him feel a little better after his Pop had died and after what had happened to Pastor Ron. Jesus also befriended the new Pastor at Abba AME Zion Church who taught Jesus how to play the keyboards. This was a new church founded by the Father, Son, and Holy Ghost and by Pastor Charles Wayne Baxter.

Pastor Baxter had a vision to do more joint projects with other churches in the community. He was really big on trying to promote what he called "community." Everything he talked about was community-this and community-that. Because he'd done an acting gig in high school, he was asked to help lead a drama at the church. One of the programs that Jesus participated in was called a *Maafa*. It was sponsored by the Harambee United Church of Christ up the road which memorialized the Middle Passage of the African slave trade, the Underground Railway, the Jim Crow Era, and the Civil Rights Movement. Jesus played a small role in the drama as a poor fugitive slave trying to escape on Harriet Tubman's Underground Railway. Everyone who went to see it thought Jesus did a convincing job as a runaway slave. He sure did cry out like a wounded hound when he was caught, beaten, and hung against a tree to be whipped like a common criminal. Jesus also appeared at the end of the production when the Civil Rights Marchers all sang together *we shall overcome!*

Pittsburgh Jesus

Most of the time, Jesus was a loner. He was pensive, intense, and some might say, moody. Who were his really close friends? He stayed close to everyone he had known from his early childhood. He kept his distance from folks kind of like how a mouse keeps his distance from a green snake lying in green grass waiting for him to make a wrong move. Don't get me wrong: Jesus was friendly enough with folks but, at the same time, he liked the warm hug of a quiet, uninterrupted silence. Most folks kept their distance from him because they thought he seemed unapproachable. They didn't know what to make of him going off alone from time to time. He probably never would've made a good politician unless he could learn to loosen up, slap folks on the back, tell silly stories, and make small talk.

Sometimes, Jesus would go off for a week at a time to try to know what it'd be like to live on the streets so he'd go and live on the streets. This was probably some idea that the priests put in his head. Brother Ned, the white guy at the Catholic Worker House, was always talking to Jesus about the homeless. But Jesus wasn't ever really sure if Brother Ned actually knew the names of any of the people that he lumped into a great category called the "the homeless." Did Brother Ned even know if they even wanted to be homeless or not? When the two of them talked, Jesus told Brother Ned that he saw things differently – that their freedom appealed to him. Maybe it was the homeless people who made the city a home for everyone else because they didn't go off behind walls and live for themselves. Maybe their home was in God's loving and merciful heart and those in houses didn't need the love and mercy of God so God was more real to the homeless than to those who weren't looking for some bread or some wine to get by for another cold night.

One time Brother Ned suggested that Jesus should spend some time walking on the Appalachian Trail. He drove Jesus over to a little town a million miles away from Harrisburg called Boiling Springs, or Boiling Wells, or something like that; where Jesus could get on the trail and begin to walk back toward town. It seemed like a good idea to Jesus. He'd first learned to camp out when he was a boy scout with scout master Billy Cramer. Mr. Billy Cramer was a boxer and a dapper dresser who was something of a role model to Jesus. He was part Indian and only got his hair cut every seven years. Billy later went on to be the Youth Director for the YMCA and touched a lot of lives. Jesus often told whoever would be listening was that the only reason that he ever left the boy scouts was to go "girl-scouting." Hahaha!

Brother Ned told Jesus about his travels to China, Nepal, northern India, Thailand and the killing fields of Cambodia. He talked about a place called the Potala Palace in Tibet and how the communist Chinese soldiers invaded Tibet and killed monks and raped the lady monks while they were conquering. He said that the Tibetans were killed for no reason and with no defense. Brother Ned said that he'd even been on a seven-day train ride all the way from Ulaan Bataar Mongolia to Moscow called the Trans-Siberian Railway. He talked about some of the Russians he'd met on the train that had lived in Mongolian huts out in the grasslands to find a loving and merciful God and meaning in life. Brother Ned said it was on that train ride that he learned to play chess the way the Russians play it. It was also where he felt called of a loving and merciful God to come back to Harrisburg and serve as a Catholic worker. Why look for the God of mercy in Mongolia or Russia when you can seek Him at your own home?

What I've always noticed is that white people know how to do charities that help other people and make a good living out of it in the process. Rich white girls become social workers, and rich white boys become missionaries who travel all over the world, or priests, or inner city school teachers before that gets too stressful to have to deal with and the romance of it all fades away a little bit. Then they can become professors or write books about all of their adventures. Jesus loved to hear stories about Brother Ned's travels around the world and especially to China. Brother Ned had told him about a month he spent in Yunnan among a group of people called the Naxi who would have the women of their village marry as many men as they wanted. Each night the women of the village would call the men whom they chosen for the night into the house while the rest of them had to wait outside until they got lucky with their lady. Brother Ned taught Jesus how to write the Chinese character for love and the way that Chinese people say hello. Asia seemed to Jesus like it was on another planet but he really liked Chinese food and wondered if he'd go there someday for a visit if he ever got enough money. Brother Ned told Jesus once that he liked Chinese food so much that maybe he was a reincarnation of one of those Tibetan nuns who were killed by the commies about the same year that his soul was being born.

There was something inside of Jesus, a holy curiosity, which really made him want to be a traveler whenever he heard Brother Ned talk about all of the places that he'd visited. He seemed driven to learn more. Jesus remembered how his Pop had told him how much he'd always wanted to travel but never did: A life of regrets and unfulfilled dreams. Jesus wanted to get out from under the suffocating blanket of the common, the mundane, the expected, and the predictable. He wanted to stretch his wings like Icarus and fly as close to the sun as he could without melting his wings. That's why the Appalachian Trail seemed like such a good idea: He took to it and kept going back to the trail to walk parts of it and to get alone and to think. Anyway, it didn't cost any money - unlike a plane ticket to Tibet. He sometimes pretended that the path would lead him to the temple of the Dalai Lama instead of to the next small nowhere town in Pennsylvania with a Dairy Queen. Jesus would ask his friends who had a car if they could drive him down to the middle of nowhere where some marker pointed to the Appalachian Trail. This wasn't something that any other brother he knew ever did, but hiking was part of the scouting culture and the trail was something that he'd heard about once on television; and hiking was something he really liked to do. It was cheap and easy and you sometimes met some interesting white folks on the trail. Most of all, it gave you the chance to be alone for long stretches of time and not see anyone or anything but trees and rocks for hours and hours at a time.

You never really knew where he'd been, but you knew he liked to be alone to think things out in his mind. Being alone helped him conjure up worlds out of his imagination. Maybe he was fighting something inside of himself? Whenever he'd come back to mama he'd tell her stories about talking to devils and temptations to have soirees with foreign looking women, to smoke pure Ganja, or to turn rocks into McDonald's Happy Meals for those who were hungry. Mama Shenice listened but thought about all of the miracles at his birth and wondered if he'd become a faith-healer or something like that. She'd listen to Jesus tell about how when he was alone in the woods he was doing acrobatics on the tops of trees and how he turned sticks into snakes. The power in the woods, he said, made him energized and able to walk across water.

His longest trip out on the Appalachian Trail lasted for about forty days. That was a serious long time to have no TV or nothing else but trees, bugs, poison-ivy, and skies. Jesus was thinking about how convoluted things were and how few folks seemed to care. He thought about violence and kids killing each other. He thought about the play he had been in about the Civil Rights movement where people weren't afraid to die for justice. Now, he thought, kids weren't afraid to kill each other just for a pair of shoes. He wanted to change something of the world's evils in his life. He wanted to go to a place in his life that he'd never been before.

Once, he stopped eating food on this hike and began to have some hallucinations. He said that as he was walking along the trail he saw the devil. I think that that old devil turned out to be a constant, ever-present adversary for the rest of his life. Whenever Jesus felt the devil, he said that he also felt a basketball team of angels all around him surrounding him and helping him out. Angels are nice to have around, he'd explain, but they usually show up only after you need them which isn't always a reassuring thought to those of us who'd never actually seen any kind of angel. Don't get me wrong, Jesus did appreciate his angels as much as the next guy; but sometimes an enemy seems to know you better than even your own friends and can help you out more than any vaporous angel ever can.

The devil got around. If the devil kept an appointment book I guess it'd be as full as the schedule of a hard-working Miami Beach hooker. I heard from a friend that our Muslim friends called him Shay-tan. Of course, Jesus had heard all about the devil but he'd never really thought that the devil would actually play a major role in trying to mess up his own life. Life always seems to come at you crazily from every direction and even the kings among us always seem to end up facing off against other kings. When Jesus saw the devil he said he felt like he was looking at the personification of evil. The stories that Mama used to read to him as a boy and all of the injustices he'd heard about at the Catholic Worker all started to come together for him. Things started to blur together. He felt like he was being pushed to do something important. Maybe he should move to the Sudan or Palestine?

The devil that Jesus talked to wasn't the devil of story-books with the red skin and the pointy tale and horns. Red? Everyone knows the devil is white anyway! The devil that Jesus faced was the devil of our hellish world that often comes into our minds like a confused professor, an amateur magician, a grumpy old, underpaid and tired clown, or a scatter-brained amateur psychologist offering insights from the most recent copy of *Psychology Today Magazine*. This devil inside of the mind of Jesus that he talked to during his long hikes in the woods was more about clumsy efforts at sidetracking the saints than about some scheming super-foe. The Devil was just "-evil" with a "D" in front and the "D" stood for death which was something that old slew-foot was all about. Jesus said that he felt like his whole life was a battle with death. Life is always a war at the border-lands when you're in exile.

The woods and the rolling, gentle mountains of Pennsylvania for him were like the way that other people talk about school or going to a university. Jesus learned from nature. But, he also needed time to embrace the natural. It was the quiet, clean air that made him feel fresh inside and stronger than when he started out on the trail. Sometimes, as he walked through the woods, he'd have energetic discussions with the devil and would often quote Holy Bible verses that his Mama had taught him when he was a little boy: *"It is written, a saint shall not live by bread alone but by every word that precedeth out of the mouth of the God of love and mercy!"* Jesus liked to quote the Bible in a loud voice. He felt like holy words were sharper than the flying swords of a Japanese Ninja or of the great Zorro.

The verse in the Holy Bible about dealing with hunger was a favorite because he knew hunger as an old friend. Fame and the desire to be great was less of an attraction for him than the idea of being able to live life and never have to worry at all about being hungry. The arrogant and the trivial fought inside his head like pinballs careening through some machine inside his head. Sometimes, however, when he'd find himself at the top of a mountain, Jesus felt the strangest urge just to throw himself from the edge of the cliff and into the valley below. There was something about letting go that seemed so much easier than constantly fighting, struggling, thinking, and trying to make sense of life all the time.

At other times, in the quiet; usually at night, it was angels, and not devils, that comforted Jesus. The world was filled with spirits. Most of them were soft, loving, women with gentle curves. The crisp silence of the skies and the stars seemed to reach into Jesus with something familiar to his soul. It felt right to feel all the moods of nature as they flowed through his soul like it was a big-city, busy greyhound bus terminal.

When Jesus was alone for those forty days he began to feel more relaxed. Some of the things that'd already happened in his life seemed clearer when he thought about them all alone in the woods. Life started to come back to him now in a three-dimensional kind of way.

The more he thought about things, the more Jesus began to see that Pastor Ron had probably been right when he talked about how people needed to get ready for the woman clothed in the sun with the moon underneath her feet and the a crown of the twelve stars. She'd need some help to fight the big red dragon with the seven heads and ten horns. It was on those trails that Jesus first volunteered to fight for that maiden against her enemy. Jesus would take up the sword and cut off the tail of that beast before he could sweep a third of the stars out of the sky and fling them to the earth.

Religion had always been in the background for Jesus because it was so central to his parents. Now, however, he started reading a Holy Bible that Pastor Ron had given him once he'd finished his confirmation after his twelfth birthday. His baptism began to mean more and more to him the more he thought about how all of the saints that he grew up with were so happy that he'd dipped under the water. The saints in his 'hood had watched out for him when he was growing up and now he felt like it was time to give back to the black community. They'd taken care of his Mama and laughed and worked with his Pop. Now, it was his turn to do something for them. He had no idea what it would be or how it'd unfold. Over time things would make more and more sense. Until then, he'd help the woman that Pastor Ron had talked about from Book of Revelations who was trying her best to flee from the raging red serpent into the wild and holy desert of protection.

Jesus began to think new ideas. Childlike convictions nurtured by family were being tested by unfamiliar voices. He was being challenged to disagree with everything that he was taught was true.

Evil had always been there; but there is something mirthful and wonderful about childhood that keeps evil from pressing its big boot too deeply into our neck. Now, evil was becoming a voice inside him – both an enemy and a friend at the same time. His mind thought about the flames of hatred and the strong currents of pleasure that drowned and distracted most people. He thought about money when he found a $100 bill beside the trail one day. He thought about a curvy, delicious, blonde, white Swedish playmate named Liv Lindeland that he first met when he found her beckoning smile in a crumpled up twenty-five year-old *Playboy* magazine, June 1972, beside the trail one day during one of his hikes.

There was so much in the ocean of the world. No one had really told him much about anything that really mattered. What was true and what wasn't true? Maybe instead of believing in fairy tales, and Santa Clauses, and a Gott Allemachtige like their parents had been teaching him, it made more sense to be a cynic and dismiss dreams as hopeless crutches for easily distracted souls. It was easier just to say that things were too complicated. People with simple faith were simpletons who should know more about how their ideas were really implausible. Thinking was a sticky spider-web. The greatest temptation that Jesus faced during those hours of thinking and being alone on the trail was the one that was the easiest to succumb to: The one of immobility. It was easier not to believe in anything and even act as if non-belief was something astute, noble, and mature. It was easier to go with the flow like a dead fish does when floating down a river. It was easier to be smug. It was easier to think that you were smarter than religious fools instead of becoming an insider and a person who didn't act so proud. It was easiest just to stay stuck in safety and live a long, quiet, easy life as a caterer or maybe as a youth pastor.

Brother Ned once told Jesus a story about how Mama pelican birds would cut their own skin with their beaks in order to feed their children. Brother Ned said that all of us should become like pelicans and feed our blood to the poor. But who wants to be a bloody pelican?

Chapter Four:
Miracles

1. Do You Believe I Can Do This?

"*Wherever he entered, in villages, cottages, or cities, they laid down their sick in the open and prayed to be allowed at least to touch the hem of his tunic; and everyone who was touched was cured.*" See Mark 1:40-43.

2. Northwest

Pittsburgh Jesus used to tell us that his friends were the greatest miracle in his life and that, once he found us, his path was set. When Jesus was about 26 or 27, in the spring of 2005, he left Harrisburg. He began to move around staying with some of his family and some brothers and sisters that he knew in Washington D. C.

Pittsburgh found a place at the Newport West Apartments on Fourteenth and Rhode Island. No place was really safe in downtown D. C. In those days, crime seemed to be on the rise. Northwest was an odd mixture of government workers, professional people, drug dealers, hustlers, and pimps. This place was right at the beginning of a hoe-stroll that went down all the way to Twelfth and K. On the upside, there was a great Jazz Club, Newport West, which was right around the corner. It was intimate, and was known for Shirley Horn, the Belle of D. C. Jazz, and also the legendary John Malachi who had once played there until he died in the 80s. You could still feel his brooding, swaying spirit of a ghost moving around the joint whenever the jams got particularly hot and heavy.

Even though Pittsburgh was new in town, he didn't start off looking for a job. Instead, he just started walking all around the 'hood and talking to people about their hopes. Even though it was dead-center in the middle of this huge city, people weren't too busy for small-talk. The brothers and sisters over there were ripe for conversations. Sometimes, Jesus said he felt like he was that guy Murray on the Fox TV show where everyone is figuring out if baby Xavon belongs to ghetto-rough David or trailer-trash Sammy; the DNA tests always seem to show that the poor kid belongs to the worst bum imaginable. Why does anyone go on these National TV shows to get slammed in the face by the steel shovel of shame?

Jesus always had time for folks. He wasn't someone who made you feel like he was in a hurry. He wasn't one of those folks who'd look over your shoulder at a party when you were talking to him, while, at the same time, he tried to act like he was interested. Pittsburgh hung out with all kinds of folks and would listen to anyone. He'd only offer his opinion when asked for it. Brothers and sisters opened up to him about all of their dramas and he'd gently talk to them about joys now and peace with the eagles in the heavens above. Other times, he'd talk to folks about the Eagles, Steelers, and Redskins - where many of us live most of the time.

The streets of any big city are full of phantoms. Jesus moved around and joined the mix. Brother Ned had told him once that Confucius had said that the best traveler makes no plans so he never worked off a schedule. That allowed him to do all kinds of random activities. Sometimes, Pittsburgh would just walk around and see some old guy trying to plant a garden or rake leaves and he'd stop and ask if he could help out. Other times, he interrupted folks washing their cars and offered to add a little elbow grease or help with the detailing. The road was always better than the Inn. I had to laugh when I saw him volunteer like this: If pappi would've ever had me volunteer to help him wash his car - which he did religiously every Sunday afternoon -he would've fallen over dead in shock.

If there was a game of street ball going on he'd jump in or, if the kids were younger, he'd stand on the sidelines and do a little coaching with them on how they could do a little better driving the lane or blocking shots. Sometimes, since folks knew him over there, Jesus volunteered to lead tours at Fredrick Douglass's house over in Southeast. He also sometimes would hang out in front the Mary McCloud Bethune house and talk to folks coming in and out about the life of our Queen Mary.

This is how Pittsburgh flowed – one day at a time. The only things he never changed was having a cup of Chinese green tea every morning while reading the letters to the editors in the Washington Post (never the Times - even when it was given to him for free!) and the sports page. He tried to keep up with the Phils and, a little bit less, with the Mets, Nats, and the woeful Pirates – the best triple-A team in the majors. He argued with some old-timers about whether his Phils were a better team than the old '75 Big Red Machine when they had Rose, Morgan, Helms, and Johnny Bench. The old-timers would call him crazy and reminded him that the Reds won 108 games in the regular season. That fact held no weight for Jesus because the Phils were the Phils and nobody was better than them - past, present, or future. That was how he rolled with his sports teams. The owner and coaches of the Steelers could never do anything wrong. He preached that the streets of heaven would be paved in gold while the sidewalks would all be black to match the colors of the Steel Curtain.

The Chinese green tea-drinking thing was weird to me because I hadn't met many brothers who loved green tea. Maybe he picked that up from his papa or from his time with Brother Ned when they'd get together and talk about China and Tibet.

Growing up in Harrisburg, Jesus was a huge Phillies fan. He was over the moon in October 2008 when they won the World Series. He always wore his Wiz Kids throwback Phils cap. Come to think of it, I never actually saw him play any baseball. He loved the history of the game and the relaxing pace. It reminded him of lazy-afternoon times with his pop, his uncles, his family, and friends.

The only thing that he played was hoops. He was a great Sixers fan until the great coach Larry Brown left and the new guy gave a bum-rap to his main man, Latrell Sprewell. Spree was eventually sold down the river to the Denver Nuggets for thirty pieces of silver. This made Latrell so mad that he got into more trouble over in Atlantic City with a fight in some VIP Strip Club or something. Man, that brother sure had some trouble in Jersey: remember when he peed in one of the fountains of one of those big Atlantic City casinos? Pittsburgh thought it wasn't fair how the NBA refs called fouls on Spree for no reason – just to put a brother in his place. Massa wanted to lynch that young buck: drag him down into the mud and make him dance to their fiddle tune. No sir, there was no one better than Latrell Sprewell in his prime: Spree was the man.

Pittsburgh had been a point guard in high school with a decent perimeter game. He stayed out of the paint. He loved his three's and took them way more than the rest of us would've liked whenever we played pick-up with him. When it came to going to pro games, Jesus didn't go to either basketball or football games because tickets were too expensive. In the summer, he went to a lot of baseball games – to see the Nationals. He'd sit in the cheapest seats that he could get and then move up after a few innings. I think he eventually got in good with some of the ushers because, every once in awhile, I'd be watching a Nats game on TV in some bar and, sure enough, you'd see his old beat-up Phillies cap right behind home-plate. Tickets to those seats probably cost an arm and a leg.

Northwest was rough. A few crews ran most of the drugs in the area. Those streets were no place for idiots who didn't know what the hell they were doing. Because the pimps were some of the best clientele that the crews had, everyone seemed to get along okay. The 'hood seemed to have at least two of everything; a modern-day Noah's Ark. There were a few transvestites, convicted pedophiles, and a few second-storey men who focused on hitting the apartments of the shut-ins because they were such an easy mark.

Northwest also had a few lawyers, retired cops, and even some politicians living in the area. They always found some time to talk with Jesus - ask him questions and seek his opinion. Pittsburgh met with a mix of folks every day for donuts around eleven just to talk. Some of the folks in Northwest made fun of his accent. His stories about hiking in the woods and mountains resulted in a few of the old folks calling him "country." That's also the first time that I heard him called "Pittsburgh" which, to these guys, was no great title of honor. They all told him that they had to teach him a thing or two about what was up and what was going down.

3. Brother Jeremy

One of the first friends Jesus made when he came to Northwest was a kid named CJ; originally from Brooklyn. He was a hustler who always had money. As it turned out, he was a dealer with some pull. CJ was a good person to know when it came to needing a little protection.

CJ introduced Jesus to one of his close friends, Brother Jeremy. The brother had once been in the Nation of Islam and, after that, the Black Panthers. Now, he was a converted Rastafarian. Jesus and Jeremy began to hang out. The brother was tall and wore African fabrics and had a beard and dreds that went down to his waist. He was a strict vegetarian. He also took every kind of vitamin and herb imaginable. In fact, you could smell a Rasta cloud of heavenly herb all over him most of the time. Jesus convinced him to start drinking Chinese green herbal tea instead of coffee. That meant that he now had someone to join him on that kick. Brother

Jeremy told us that the Rasta were predicting that Jah was about to send an end-time prophet to shake things up. The brother explained that this prophet wouldn't be a politician, or a priest, but a mystic teacher. Rasta prophesied that this prophet would be recognized by his African fabrics and wild, nappy hair as well as by sharp Zion words. Pittsburgh clearly fit the bill in terms of the words and the clothes.

Brother Jeremy was a traveler, or, as he liked to say; a pilgrim. He told some amazing stories about some of the roads that he'd gone down over the years. Rastas believed that every person you met on the road is a child of Jah God. There is no place for bitterness or hatred for anyone. In the last times, Jah God had sent the Haile Sellaise Ras Tafari to make it rain in Jamaica and to guide us all back to the light from dark Babylon.

The Brother told us his story: papa walked out on his mama and his family. After the brother got married his wife cheated on him with a white guy; and that was just the start of it. He was cool about what she did because folks can only act out of their basic natures. If someone acts like a dog then don't get upset if you hear that dog bark. But Rasta can change a dog into a King. We need to follow the "Better Zion Way" and give everyone the benefit of the doubt even when they do something stupid. Instead of forgiving, some of the sad stories he told us, made me want to knock some heads around.

If ever you got Brother Jeremy started on the Rasta way you better have a cool glass of something to drink and not be in a hurry. He would take his sweet time and lay out the message for you like a white accountant details a tax return or like how a Cholo from Atzalan details his ride. Brother Jeremy told us we needed to escape "Them Belly Full" Babylon Whore. We needed to *skuffle* down to Trench Town (since Back-O-Wall had been destroyed) on Paradise Island. Brother Jeremy went there and danced all night long; dancing to some steady drums around a bonfire of old car tires at a *Kumina* and learn some *Pukumina* word-magic mixed with Zion Jah truth. His time in the Islands empowered him to come back into the Whore of Babylon as a *Natty Dread* to do revolutionary judo. He wanted to be a lifeguard rescuing brothers and sisters drowning in the Whore of Babylon's brimming toilet.

Brother Jeremy explained to us that the Lord Jesus Christ was a black Messiah who came in the flesh with a flag of Red, Black, and Green to free people everywhere oppressed by the white man. The Everlasting black Jah would bring His princes and princesses out of Egypt and return them back to Ethiopia. Like I told you before, the Holy King was Jah Ras Tafari who came to earth with the name Haile Selassie because he roared like a mighty lion of the tribe of Judah.

Ras Tafari would come to Babylon and free Mumia Abu Jamal and the Indian Leonard Peltier. Then Ras Tafari would lead an army of Israelite locksmen with nappy dreads into the Promised Land. He'd have webbed feet of bronze and hair like the wool of a sheep. Someday, the invincible emperor would conquer the inferior devil ones. Jah would rule the world so a hopeless hell would become a heaven for all people, animals, herbs, and all other life-forms. Until the 72nd House of Power came into reality, all of us exiles shouldn't become dismayed. No trouble; no mind. According to Brother Jeremy all of I-and- I needed to stay united as one in a mood of *I-tal* or *Illalu* where a brother or sister of the Twelve Tribes should drink a lot of fruit juices and stay away from stuff like chemical soap and shampoo and from eating pork, snails, shellfish, bottom-feeders, and any big fish without scales.

4. Manoj Kampoor

Another brother that Jesus met was a gay Hindu named Manoj. He had a heart of gold but wasn't the most talkative guy you'll ever meet. Manoj's sister, Shivangi, had met Jesus and told him that she wanted him to meet her brother. Manoj hated his job and hoped to start school but Shivangi said he needed some motivation to get started again in the right direction. The two of them went by a hack out to Manoj's place of work, an area Coca-Cola Bottling plant out on the B-W Expressway.

Jesus found Manoj on the assembly line and simply shouted to him: *"Get out of here and take a break with me. I am with Shivangi here and we wanted to talk with you."*

Over the noise of the machines Manoj yelled to the stranger with his sister: *"Not now, man, I'm busy. Can't you see that this damn machine is broke?"*

"Try again with your sprocket to loosen that other bolt over there," Jesus advised.

Manoj looked at the stranger with astonishment: *"Man, I've been trying all day to get this Mo*-Fo* machine working and nothin's gonna Mo*-Fo* work. I've been at this Mo*-Fo* machine for eleven Mo*-Fo* years and now your gonna come up in here and tell me how to do my Mo*-Fo* job?!"*

"Just try again. Have any other ideas?"

"Okay – but it'll never Mo*-Fo* work." Manoj fiddled with the bolt that Jesus pointed out. He tried again to turn on the machine. It was strange.

The whole thing was some kind of a dream going on in matrix-style slow motion. This time the machine began to work smoothly for the first time in hours. *"Ganeesh! Man! How in the Mo*-Fo*hell did you know to do that?"*

Jesus explained: *"Things are easy when you hear a loving and merciful God speak to you. You are a miracle waiting to happen my brother. Now, pack up your tools and come with Shivangi and me out for a coffee. What doesn't happen is sometimes more important than what does!"*

Manoj couldn't describe what was going on in his mind when he met Jesus. Everything Jesus said made sense and he didn't have to use any arguments to get his point across. That's how Pittsburgh was with what he had to say: short, and sweet, and to the point. It wasn't what he said, anyway, but how he said it, and how the force of his example left an impression.

Manoj packed his tools and agreed to go for coffee. He began to follow Jesus and never went back to that damned assembly line.

5. John Francis and Charlie

There were about ten or twelve of us who hung out with Jesus in D. C. We may have all been rich in potential but not much else. We were both his friends and his bodyguards. None of us were really tied down to very much except a few petty debts.

One guy who sometimes showed up was Charlie, a Baptist preacher. He was a hard person to read. You never really knew whose side he was on or what he was all about. He was old but had never gotten married. Charlie always groused about generating smart alternatives for welfare and getting rid of low housing rates. He supported a left-wing politician named Ralph Nader and always told us Nader's ideas about complex environmental, economic, and political issues.

The rest of us, like Pittsburgh, were big Obama fans. Most of us were black and poor but there was myself, a local Cubano, and this short Irish white guy, a street musician from Philly named John Francis who hung around with us. He drank a lot of rum and coke. We called him "John the Radical" or simply *Rad* for short. If Rad hadn't been so tight with his money or so worried about it all the time you might not have even known he was white.

Rad wanted to be a *race traitor*. He was really hard on white people and was always bringing up stuff about racism when the rest of us really didn't want to talk about it. Jesus said there actually was only one race - the human race. He never checked any government form or census paper that asked for his "race" but always checked the "other" box and wrote in "human." High-minded arguments about racism in America didn't change who was in prison or who was hassled by the police. Talk didn't change the fact that most African-Americans hung out, and married, other African-Americans and most Cubanos, like me, hung out and married other Cubanos. The same was true for most white folks.

John Francis was okay in my book. One time Rad gave me a book about a Cuban writer named Armando Valladares. When I told pappi about the book he told a story of how Valladares boldly criticized Castro even though Fidel had sent the guy to a prison island for twenty years called the Ilos de Pinos. It was nice of Rad to give me that book. The kid was a decent song-writer and the rumor was that he'd once worked for the IRS. He was a strange guy but he played some interesting music. It was good we knew him because he had some connections in Philly that helped us out once all the trouble started.

Speaking of books, Pittsburgh carried around the poetry of Nikki Giovanni. He was trying to memorize her poems. Another friend, Iya Isoke, got Jesus interested in this lady's poetry. Jesus could recite from memory a poem called "Beautiful Black Men with Compliments and Apologies to all not Mentioned by Name."

One book that Jesus and Rad read together, and argued about, was called *Yurugu*. It was pretty intense. Reading a page felt like swimming across the everglades at night in a business suit. The premise was that Europeans had created the field of anthropology to study Africans, and Indians to prove that they were barbaric. The book title came from a term in one of the African languages for white folks; "*Yurugu*", which actually means "*restless ghosts*" because these Africans observed how stressed out the whites were about everything. The black author claimed that Europeans promoted power-seeking as a high virtue. She reasoned that Europeans prized science and materialism and scorned the spiritual. They felt it was their duty to impose their enlightened values on inferior others; the same way that social workers try to "help" us today.

Whatever the skin color of Jesus and all of us, what we shared in common was that all of our wallets were empty of green. Most of us were unemployed. One guy, Cedric, quit his job when he met us. Jesus met Cedric while he was on a work-crew repaving a section of the Suitland Parkway. Jesus! Seems like they were always working on that road! Pittsburgh came up to Ced and said "*Follow me, friend, and I'll help you pave a road that helps folks enter the Kingdom of a loving and merciful God.*

Every brother or sister has to decide how they gonna live their own lives. That's up to each of us."

Cedric dropped his tools right there and then. Boy! Was his boss pissed when he walked away.

6. My Story

Jesus interrupted me while I was selling t-shirts with my brother Tristan. He invited me to take a break and sit down and have a donut. Who could say no to a Boston Crème? I never went back to Tristan's t-shirt stand again. It wasn't like, the first time that I met Jesus, that he hit me with a bolt of lightning or anything.

Caesar Chavez Garnica grew up as a decent Cubano kid in D. C. My mama was really into religion- the Holy Roman Catholic and Apostolic Faith – and she prayed for us every day. Pappi worked constantly. I hardly ever saw him except when he came home late at night to smoke a cigar and watch boxing on TV. Mama loved the Virgin Mary of Guadalupe more than she loved pappi and the rest of us combined. She was really big on her rosary. I never understood why that was so important to her. I married a Catholic girl – Isabella – when I was only 19. That sure was a mistake! I was divorced after seven years of pure hell. Anyway, the good thing about my marriage was it forced me into an honest job and I never really got into much trouble like some of the other kids that I grew up with.

My ex-wife was super religious and, like mama, was also really big on God and the Blessed Mother. I grew up with pictures all around our house of the Virgin Mary of Guadalupe, of St. Joseph, Padre Pio, and of the Lord Jesus Christ. The Lord Jesus Christ in these pictures looked like some blonde-haired blue-eyed gringo with shoulder-length brownish-blond hair who wanted to collect on a debt. The nuns at school said that the Lord Jesus Christ would help you if you were good but, the way I saw it, He was mostly helping out a lot of white people who lived a pretty easy life because they had everybody working for them. The Lord Jesus Christ spoke Hebrew, wore sandals, and had a white robe with a blue sash. It all seemed a little gay. In the pictures He also carried a long stick to push sheep around.

The priest at our church, Father Miguel Rivera, explained that the Lord Jesus Christ came to the earth to do miracles in little villages and give sermons on the sides of mountains before He died on the cross for our sins and came alive again from the dead so He could ascend into heaven. The Jesus that I knew as a friend, however, was far less holy than the heavenly version that Father Miguel worshipped or that mama spent so much time praying to. The Lord Jesus Christ was nothing like a poor, black, or Hispanic man; Jesus Scott was so normal that you probably couldn't spot him in a busy crowd.

7. First Run in with the Cops

Early on our posse of friends gained the attention of the local police. Maybe this had to do with the fact that CJ was a known dealer. CJ joked that he should begin to use an alias to get out from under the rough reputation he'd already made for himself. Jesus was listening: *"CJ – my brother- you should now be called the Rock because a great mansion is going to be built on the shoulders of your life."* After that, we sometimes called CJ –*The Rock* – like that huge, tough guy in the action movies.

After Jesus had been in D. C. for about a year, the cops came out of nowhere and picked him up for some questioning. We were with him when they came. We'd had a late start that morning because our hooker friend Alexis made a delicious French-toast and eggs brunch for us while Pittsburgh was watching the movie *Titanic* again.

For some reason, the man loved that movie. He thought Leonardo di Caprio was a great actor. He loved the scene where Leonardo gambled to win the tickets from Ireland to America. After the movie was over, and, after we washed the dishes, all of us walked toward Logan Circle. Over near there, a group of old white folks picked up trash from alongside the street every Saturday afternoon. Someone said we should go over and help them that day as we'd done on other weekends. The lady who ran this group was an old hippie and the name of the group was called the *Local Green Team*. Those folks sure appreciated it when the ten of us showed up to add our muscle to help them out for an hour or so.

This is how it went down: A tall white cop came up to Jesus and was showing his nightstick as if Jesus was gonna make a run for it or something. They said that they were on the lookout for a middle-aged black male who'd robbed a local 7-11. When this man was confronted, he shot the night-manager through the head and killed him. They were looking for a big middle-aged black man and Jesus Scott fit that description. The first thing the cop said was: *"Excuse me- can you step over here please?"*

Instinctively, I stepped between Jesus and this Bull Connor: *"What's going on Mr. Officer?"*

The cop looked sternly at me and said nothing. He turned to Jesus and barked out in a sharp but very controlled voice, *"Do NOT talk unless I tell you to talk. Do not move. Put your hands up high in the air where I can see them. Now, do you have any ID on you, Sir?"*

Pittsburgh moved in careful, slow motion. His father had taught him what to do in this situation. He stayed as cool as the other side of the pillow. A brother had to be careful if the man in front of him had an itchy trigger-finger: *"Yes, Sir, it's in my back pocket."*

The police officer barked more instructions: *"Continue to keep your hands up in the air. Don't move even an inch. Are there any syringes or blades in your pockets that might poke me when I search?"*

Jesus looked at him straight in the eye for a moment and then whispered sadly: *"No sir."*

For some reason, this pause, or the glance in his eyes infuriated the already-jumpy officer: *"Listen pal, don't get testy with me. Don't act like a smart-ass! I don't have the patience for it today."*

With his hands still high up in the air still Jesus began:*"Look, Sir, I didn't mean any disresp—"*

"That's it. Get in the car." The cop spun Pittsburgh around. He pushed him over to his squad car. I remember, for some reason, that the officer driving that squad car was listening to a Kirk Franklin CD called the *New Nation Project;* that was surreal. Everybody knew what could happen to a black male once a white cop got a notion that he was *acting up*. We all prayed for Jesus that night. Most cops were okay but you never could tell about some folks once they put on a blue uniform; it was if they were back in 'Nam or Afghanistan among the savages with a renewed license to kill. As it turned out, the cops just kept Pittsburgh overnight, asked some questions, and then let him go free before dawn.

"What do you think – should we follow him to the precinct?" The Rock asked me after the squad car began to speed away. No: better just to wait. He'd know where to find us when he came out. There might be trouble if we went to the station. Nothing good could come from a gang showing up and asking questions. None of us looked respectable or talked smoothly; except maybe for Rad. We decided to sit tight and not try to get mixed up in this problem.

When Pittsburgh got back from the precinct we were waiting at the donut shop. He ordered a Boston Crème and sat down with Brother Jeremy to have some Chinese green herbal tea. The rest of us sipped at our coffees and ate our donuts just like we always did as if nothing had happened out of the ordinary. I had an apple-fritter that day. Jesus told us that it was all resolved because the officer who had brought him in had gone out and found another big, young black man who they decided to book him for the murder instead. This other kid was part of a gang, had dropped out of school, and had refused to join the army. It was a sure bet: Nobody would miss this little punk; guilty or innocent. They let Jesus go. They took his fingerprints and some pictures so that they could open a file on him for the future. One of the cops told Jesus that he didn't appreciate his smug know-it-all attitude and didn't like his dreds, his name, or the company he kept. Sooner or later, the cop warned, there would be a reason for them to meet again.

Another officer pulled Jesus aside before he was released, and vividly described to him what it'd be like when he was arrested again; how he'd be gang-raped in a maximum-security prison. This was some pretty sick, twisted humor. The way Pittsburgh told it, this officer was a tall white guy with Maori tattoos all over his arms. He told Jesus that he was "looking forward" to the day when he'd personally tie him down onto an electrocution table or end his life with a legally prescribed cocktail of lethal poisons. This cop laughed as he described how slowly somebody dies when those drugs are working their way through you like a lazy snake and how the volts of electricity would make his Afro fray up and frizzle like Bozo the Clown. Pittsburgh just sat there and said nothing.

That was all that Jesus told us about what happened while he'd been held overnight for questioning.

We figured that, sooner or later, we'd probably have more trouble with the cops. Thinking this way helped us prepare for the worst while still hoping for the best. Northwest was too much like some apocalyptic scenes out of *Blade Runner* to think that we could be immune. Since everyone on the street heard about Jesus being taken in, we began to hear about all kinds of rumors about how Jesus had raped Manoj, his gay follower, or Big Sheena, our lesbian sister. Other folks guessed that we paid for our pizza and donuts by selling crack to kids on the playground. Another rumor whispered that a corrupt cop only let Pittsburgh free after he'd paid a drug-money bribe. Some of the pillars of the community – as well as the cops - became convinced that Pittsburgh was hiding some secrets. Sooner or later, this man would get caught. Then, we'd all learn the real story.

8. New York City Subways

We decided that, because of the police-scene, it'd be best if we moved up to New York City for a while. We weren't running away but a temporary move would make our lives easier in some ways. Mostly, it was Rock's idea. He arranged for us to stay with some of his friends and his former mother-in-law, Mrs Palovitch, who he was still very close with. Rock knew people all over the place – Queen's, Brooklyn, the Bronx, Staten Island, and Harlem. He even had family up in Mt. Vernon and around White Plains.

Mrs. Palovitch, Rock's former mother-in-law, had a massive house with plenty of room for all of us in the Washington Heights part of Brooklyn. He explained that nobody would bother us at this house because there was a rumor that it was haunted and that old lady Palovitch used to catch little kids and cook them alive for her Jewish rituals. Mrs. Palovitch also had a gun and had waived it more than once to folks lingering in front of her house. Pittsburgh agreed with the plan: *"Let's go somewhere else for awhile since other folks need to hear what we're saying."* We ended up in NYC for about a year.

New York had such a different kind of a vibe than Northwest. It was also more expensive since we had less folks helping us out financially. Pittsburgh panhandled at subway stations and asked Rad to play a few anti-war songs with his open guitar case. We got a little money for food that way. Sometimes, when Rad finished a song Jesus would start shouting: *"In God's Kingdom there are no races or divisions of folks. All of us are children of God; we all need grace. There should be no hatreds made by divisions here on earth. Can't you read the graffiti on the wall? If one of our brothers or sisters is hurting, then all of us are hurting. Do not covet the goods or the wives of your neighborhood. If your leg gets cut and starts to bleed doesn't your hand reach down and try to mend your cut?"* Sometimes Jesus got so deep into his preaching to the crowds that he forgot to ask for money at the end of his spiel.

Once, at a certain subway station, we heard this crazy man asking folks to push him into the path of an oncoming train. He was a big, large dark-skinned middle-aged man who told folks that he'd once been born a prince in Igboland, West Africa. That was about all he ever said.

Nobody ever saw this prince sleep around that station. Maybe when he closed his eyes or dreamed, he was back in his home jungle with huge ants and hungry hyenas eating at his flesh. Maybe in his mind, Prince was always hunting in some African jungle for owls or grubs or whatever hunters eat over there. Maybe there was a curvy woman somewhere lost in his past. Maybe Prince was drinking water out of putrid skulls or living in a tent made of animal bones. Who knows? The man was crazy.

The big African always wore a Grateful Dead t-shirt no matter what the weather. This probably explains why he was always coughing like he had some advanced case of tuberculosis. Some of us guessed that Prince probably had a multiple-personality disorder or some other kind of chemical imbalance in his brain. Prince told folks his name sometime but it was in some African tongue and it was hard to pronounce and even harder to remember. One thing was certain, day and night, Prince basically lived in that subway station while everyone else just tried to steer around him and avoid him.

The day that Pittsburgh met Prince he'd been walking around the station begging for folks to push him in front of an oncoming train. Evidently, Prince asked folks to do this for him often although no one talked with him because he was as wild as a pigeon trapped in a mailbag. Pushing this African into an on-coming train was clearly a bad idea for all involved.

The only thing that folks did was run from Prince's errant coughs which sounded like the kiss of death to anyone who heard them or might get in their toxic way. The man saw Pittsburgh and began to move in his direction. For a second, the Rock thought the African was going to try to tackle Jesus so he tried to get in front of him. Instead, when Prince got near Jesus his face twisted up and he shouted in a really strange voice: *"Have you come to destroy us? Oynise! Eze! Why are you here? Leave us alone."*

Prince had the strange ability to speak with different voices like a ventriloquist can do on TV. His voice sounded like the horrible machine-gun rattle of an army of hornets. He seemed like someone who had no mama and seemed as lost as a blind goose in a blizzard. Jesus knew that these different voices - coming out of one mouth - were lying; none of them were the voice of this beaten-up old Igbo prince.

Pittsburgh looked around at the crowd and shouted: *"Listen up New York! The Lord your God Almighty – the Lord is One- Oldamare, Allah of the Hausa, Oluwu of the Yoruba, the Chineke and the Eze and the Chukwu of our Igbo brother-The Lord is One! Here are commands for you today: Love the Lord of mercy and love with all of your heart mind and soul! Love your homeless sisters and brothers backed up against a wall like you would love yourself or like you'd love a famous Brazilian supermodel!"*

Pittsburgh turned to Prince and quietly put his hand on his shoulder: "What is your name?"

Prince looked at him:"*My name is Ndi Nmadu Chine because I am a big market-crowd. Please don't send me back to the Okumo. What do you want *from us Jesus of the Streets? Please send me into a flock of nnunu or into a pack of nketa. At least they'll eat bugs and make nests of trash like we love."*

Jesus interrupted: *"From now on you are my Nwane Nwoke. From now on you will be on a new path to Emigwe and you will find your own way back home again to your father and to all of our Biafran ancestors. Fear is no longer your food and your drink. You are the Prince. Follow me, my older brother."*

All of us also followed as Jesus led Nwane Nwoke out of the station and up into the street. We came out near Pier 17 and the river. Jesus walked over to a nearby park bench with the man and sat him down. The park was filled with seagulls that scattered. Pittsburgh thundered at the man: *"The God of love and mercy wants to give you a clear mind. Be healed brother, your sins are forgiven and you are free from your confusion."* The man changed in a way that you can't really explain. It all happened so fast.

At the same time that Nwane Nwoke was healed, all of the sea-gulls in the park started to go ballistic. Some of them flew into buildings and some of them flew straight up into the air like fireworks or straight down smashing into the sidewalk and dying in a really gruesome way to watch-- splat!

After about three or four minutes of this, things finally calmed down except for some very angry white park cleaners who were looking at all of the mess of the birds and shouting at us: *"Get out of here ya troublemakers! Look what you've done here! Who's going to clean up this damn mess of all of these dead birds?"* It was all too confusing. The real fact was that they had to clean up hundreds of dead birds. All they wanted to do was to finish up a boring day at work and go home to watch the Yankees.

When Nwane Nwoke looked to thank Pittsburgh he had already vanished into the busy crowd along the street. We didn't find him until we got back to the Palovitch house about two hours later.

9. The Crack House

The next day, Jesus, Ced, Rad, the Rock, Charlie, and I went into a crack house where the Rock had done a lot of business before he met us in D. C. Everyone at first was looking at Rad with suspicion until the Rock said that he was okay. Jesus started talking with Renee, a beautiful, beautiful sister who was now turning tricks to make her addiction and to pay for her expensive makeup and braids.

Renee had been on a long toll-road in life. She'd started out as one of those girls who'll never do anything wrong. She'd cry if she thought she was disappointing her parents in any way. She graduated and went to one of those small Christian colleges in Pennsylvania out in the country and was doing okay there until she realized that she didn't belong and never wanted to belong there. When she cried out for help, the folks around her didn't know what to do. So, instead of just loving her, they quoted the Holy Bible and prayed for demons to come out of her. Some folks are so plastic that when they try to help they actually make you feel much worse than when they started. Her Christian classmates talked a good Holy Bible game, wore Jesus T-shirts, W. W. J. D. bracelets, and all wanted to be social work majors so they could go out into the real, scary world and help poor black and Hispanic kids. They were self-assured and insular. Renee was never just a sister in Christ. She was always a black actress on the info-tainment margins of their white little pre-real world Alice-in-Wonderland Tea Party. Why had she given up the bands and fun of Morgan State to come north for this? What in the world had she been thinking?

The dam broke. Renee dropped out of that safe, warm little Christian college bubble. In the long run, that was probably a mistake. At first, she was just going to parties and having fun. Before long, a boyfriend got Renee mixed up with crack. The water-slide went fast and furious straight down from there. She was wounded and vulnerable. Everyone asked about her body but nobody asked about the dreams she had conjured up when she was a little girl. Her friends were no real friends at all. One of her so-called boyfriends even stalked her and tried to run her over with his car in a grocery store parking lot!

Over time, Renee started getting late on her rent payments for her apartment. One of her boos offered to help her get a little more money in exchange for some loving. She felt so dirty after that so she turned to the pure, white snow to dull the pain and take away the ugly feeling inside. She wondered if there was any light in the world. It was no longer just one problem that she tried to heal with her white snow, but one problem after another, until she was under an avalanche of feelings that held her mind hostage.

The powder took over. It became her family and all that mattered to Renee. Her days became cold sweats and miserable cravings. Folks around her used her up and filled her with their left-over garbage. She fell to the earth so many times that every time she took one step forward, she'd take seven steps backwards. There was no more present moment. There was nothing left that she controlled. All she wanted was relief from pain. Renee needed some amniotic fluid around her to protect her like she used to have when she had been inside the womb. None of that was there for her anymore except in the crack. The crack was her mother's nipple and her mother's body. It was her skill-set and her education. It was her alpha and omega. She desired the crack and the crack desired her: a sad game. What didn't happen in her life should have happened. Everything inside of her was unfinished and neglected. There was no more satisfaction. Renee became a hungry ghost.

When Pittsburgh started into his standard love and happiness speech to Renee one of the other crack-heads named Darius shouted: *"Man, get the f*** out of here! We aint got time for this fake holy Bullsh-**!"* Jesus looked over at us by the doorway: *"What people have been doing to try and help these people hasn't worked. It's never going to work. We need to change the whole approach. Tinkering around the edges of these problems will only rearrange the furniture but never make a real difference. Cases like this require prayer and fasting."*

Jesus had connected in some way with Renee. She was at the end of her rope and was pulling him into herself. She looked up: *"Can you make me clean?"* Was she coming on to him? Was it a joke? Or, was this something else going on?

Pittsburgh was reading my thoughts: *"Love changes any and every equation. Why do people despise addicts? We ostracize them because we don't want them to be a mirror that shows us how much we resemble them. People trying to find the American Dream will find that it is not only futile; but also self-destructive. It destroys everything it touches and kills anything of the truth. The reason is simple: Life is about giving and not getting. People with an empty heart are looking to play a trump card and to find the queen of hearts in every poker hand. Love suffocates enemies like this woman's emptiness into submission by its force. But love is always a decision and it is an action and never just some feeling or some idea. Lovers need, and give love, while bitter people can only spread their bitterness or their sense of hopelessness."*

Jesus turned to Renee: *"Your pipe is already broken. You've just been healed from your need my dear little sister. Be free from pursuing that which you can never find. No more willful blindness. Come with us -let's get outta here."* A Cheshire cat smile came over her face. That smile made her look five years younger in a second. Later, Renee told us that when Jesus said this to her, she suddenly felt like all of her blood inside of her body was brand new like she'd just had a total transfusion. She felt new inside; fresh and clean, like how she felt before she began turning tricks. Renee walked out of there and never went back into another crack house.

That afternoon we were trying to make sense of what happened. Jesus pulled out four twenty dollar bills out of his pocket that Darius had given him at the crack house. He suggested that we all go down to the Bed-Stuy Fish Fry to celebrate the twists and turns of a good day with some golden scallops and clams.

10. The New York Aquarium

One Sunday afternoon, instead of going to church at Riverside to hear Dr. Forbes preach, Jesus suggested that we go over to the New York Aquarium since a guest speaker had been scheduled for that week. I'd never been to an aquarium before.

They have every kind of fish you can possibly imagine. In one hallway you can see sharks, stingrays, and barracuda flying over your head as you walk down a long corridor. They had starfish and some really creepy fish with fluorescent eyes that only live in the darkest parts of the ocean. I definitely want to go there again sometime.

Right in the middle of this amazing shark-tank display some of the white workers in the aquarium came up to us. Believe it or not, they were actually carrying one of their friends – I'll call him Bud - on an old sofa. They said that they'd heard about the miracle that'd happened to Renee after she met Pittsburgh. When they saw him show up at the aquarium out of the blue they felt like they just had to run over to Bud's house and bring him down to the aquarium to ask Jesus to pray for him to get a miracle like the one that Renee had experienced. These friends were really serious about helping their buddy because they had already taken Bud to one Pentecostal healing service after another.

Bud really needed help. What had happened to Bud was that he had been working at a metal-stamping factory and had accidently been pushed into a stamping machine while it was running. The accident quickly crushed his two legs and one of his arms. Bud had been lucky he hadn't been killed altogether. But, he'd been paralyzed ever since. Jesus looked at Bud: *"Young brother – your sins are forgiven!"*

As soon as Pittsburgh said that Bud jumped up out from the sofa and started to shout, sing, and praise God in front of the shark tank. The other folks in the aquarium thought that what was going on must've been some kind of show that was being put on but they couldn't figure out what it was or how it could relate to sharks and stingrays. Everyone was stunned except Charlie who asked Jesus: *"How can you forgive a person of their sins?"* That is what Charlie said. Jesus also sensed that Charlie probably didn't like the fact that the guy who was healed was a white brother. Charlie had some serious issues.

Jesus responded: *"Which is easier to say? Your sins are forgiven or, get off that sofa, be healed, and go home?"*

Sometimes, such as in that instance, Pittsburgh seemed a little harsh with Charlie. But, in all fairness to Charlie, the whole thing – happening at the New York Aquarium was a little strange to begin with. Talking about forgiving sins was also a little bit high off the charts. Maybe Jesus was angry at Charlie, not for the question, but for asking it at all at a point when somebody who'd really been messed up had finally gotten a miracle. Bud sure was happy that day. I'll never forget the look on his face when he first jumped out of that sofa in that huge shark hall as long as I live.

11. Kenig's Delicatessen

While in New York we often went as a group to a deli down by the Guggenheim Museum. They used to give us free food and always gave us free coffee. We found it because Jesus loved to go down to the Guggenheim and pass a few hours looking at the paintings. One specific painting in New York that he loved was at the Whitney Museum. It was a picture of a mother and his son by some guy named Arshile Gorky. Jesus also loved the paintings of Mark Rothko at the Guggenheim which, to me, just looked like big squares of random colors. I didn't get it. It was a little more interesting when Jesus explained how this Jewish guy Rothko had eventually killed himself and how he hated to make art that was only to be seen by rich people who paid him to paint his stuff.

The name of the deli that we usually stopped at was called Kenig's Deli. No matter what we ordered the owner would always double our order so it was a great way for us to save some money. Howard, the owner, said he tried to remember the name of every person who came into his deli by name. There was another deli down in Philly, Koch's, where the guy there did exactly the same thing with everyone who came into the shop. Howard Kenig certainly didn't make much money off of us with all of his free samples and extras but we sure weren't complaining. Generosity is a rare and wonderful thing.

One time Jesus was talking with Howard, he began to fret about the health of his ten year old daughter. Rebecca was dying of a rare form of bone cancer that nobody seemed to be able to control. Howard was unmarried and his who life was his deli and his only daughter. The cancer had started when she was still a baby. Howard and Rebecca had visited

Mt. Sinai so many times he felt like he knew everyone there including the cleaning staff. They'd had years of chemo and special treatments; nothing had worked. So many treatments that led to nowhere also cost Howard so much money that, now, he didn't honestly know if he could afford yet another round of costly experiments or if his daughter's soul could recover from yet another round of crushed hopes. Howard pleaded with Pittsburgh: "*Some people say you have new-age healing powers. If so, I need some help and I'm willing to try anything. My daughter needs a miracle. Do you think she can ever be healed?*"

Pittsburgh asked to go back alone with Howard on the PATH train to his apartment at the edge of Hoboken. The two men didn't talk much on the train. Going into the apartment, Howard noticed and appreciated the fact that Jesus also touched the mezuzah at the doorway. This apartment was cluttered beyond belief and was filled to the brim with Howard's philosophy and science books. A wheelchair was folded up in the corner. Jesus was only in the apartment for a few minutes. When he met Rebecca he closed his eyes and prayed a blessing for her in Hebrew. That's what Howard said afterwards. Jesus then said goodbye and excused himself to catch another train back across the river. That was all.

How in the world that a kid from the 'hood knew some Hebrew was beyond me. Maybe that part was an embellishment from Howard's wishful imagination. You never know.

We later learned that, the next week, when Howard took Rebecca to Mt. Sinai for a check-up the doctors called them both in to tell them, although they could not explain how, that all of the cancer was gone. It was a miracle; there was no other explanation.

12. Vietnam Vet

One day, Pittsburgh noticed a dignified older man walking with a cane toward the community center near Mrs. Palovitch's house. Leo Stapelton often stopped outside the center to tell anyone who would listen stories about the Vietnam War.

Leo was in the fifth U. S. infantry, company B, second platoon. Their name was the "bobcats" and their motto was "I'll try, Sir!" It wasn't long before he was no longer an "F. N. G." As one of Nixon's hired guns, Leo fought through Cu Chi, in the Hobo, and at the Citadel. He had seen his friends go down – Roger Leroy Coffman, our squad leader from Columbus, Ohio who died in Tay Ninh. There was Randall Lee Ellis, from Justice, West Virginia, another squad leader; and Francis William

Pittsburgh Jesus

Harter who were all killed in the same ambush. He remembered David Hensel; his friend Ronald Di Bartolomeo, from a town called Volant near Pittsburgh. Ronald was killed at Bien Hoa. He remembered Clyde Wesley Lawrence from Oklahoma City who died in Cambodia. He remembered Jose Ramon Sandoval of Colorado who was killed at Long Khan. Not a day went by when he did not recite their names or recall their faces to memory. These men did their duty. Only those of us who came back, Leo said, could understand what these people experienced; they were true heroes. Folks had no idea what was going on over there in those damned god-forsaken little rice paddies: No idea.

Leo talked a lot about an R and R place called Vung Tau where he used to swim and lounge on the beach meeting some beautiful Vietnamese women. Even the rats in Vung Tau looked more handsome than the ones around his R. P. G. Leo said the sky in Nam was so blue; the grass was so green; but, sometimes, the nights were so black that you could not see an inch in front of your face.

Leo always talked about one Sunday morning: He had been assigned to go on a mission into a valley whose name he couldn't pronounce. It turned out to be the worst day of his life. After a half hour, the copter descended into a field. He jumped out. He can still hear the sound of the chopping of the helicopter blades. In a second, something hits him and knocks him to his feet. He hears a tornado wssshh through the jungle like the moaning of a monster. He sees a flash of orange and, then, everything went black. Friends resist a spray of steel to drag him into a ditch until another chopper can get him out of there. The sky all around was blossoming with shells. Finally, Leo fell unconscious. Everything went silent. The next day he woke up in a hospital back at Vung Tau.

Have you ever known somebody blind? It can be a pretty depressing sight. I knew someone in my 'hood growing up. Blind folks are actually pretty amazing people. They have their own books with bumps and dashes instead of words on the paper. They can do all kinds of things that you'd never expect. Some blind folks can even do some things that people who can see cannot do. They may not be able to see but some blind folks can tell you when an ant is crawling up a blade of grass next to them. They notice stuff through smell, touch, intuition, or something that most of us never see all around us.

Pittsburgh switched the subject of the conversation from the Vietnamese women on the beaches of Vung Tau to the fact of Leo's blindness: *"Mr. Stapleton, do you mind if I ask you a question? Do you believe a loving and merciful God can heal you of your blindness?"* Wow! That sure came out of the blue like a bolt of lightning.

Leo stopped and drew his breath with slow intentionality. Who knows what was going on in his mind? Maybe he was thinking of his beautiful mother's face which, maybe, he saw in front of him all the time. Perhaps he didn't want to see her wrinkles that he felt with his hands, but only to hold in his eyes what he held in his heart. Maybe the mud in Leo's world was purple and the trees were all shades of yellow and gold. Why give that up for what is true and boring and real and sometimes sad and decaying and falling apart like an inner-city ghetto? Maybe Leo, through Vietnam's gift of blindness, lived in another world. Maybe in his valiant, frozen world he could see the smiles of Sandoval, Coffman, Ellis, Harter, Lawrence, Hensel, and DeBartolmeo, just like he saw them in the spring of 1971. Maybe being healed would mean he'd have to leave the world that he had come to know and rejoin the rest of us.

It seemed like a minute of silence. Finally, Leo answered: *"Son, anything is possible. I have seen it all in my life, so nothing would surprise me now. There must be some kind of a merciful God, otherwise I wouldn't be here. And, I guess He can do whatever He wants to do."* Jesus touched Leo and things started to change for him right away after over 30 years of blindness. *I can see people but they look like palm trees. It looks like the palm trees are walking, while the people seem to be losing their leaves.*

It was actually happening – Leo was beginning to see for the first time since Nam. When I heard what Leo said about mixing trees up with people, I thought about how, when I was a kid, I used to see dragons and horses in the shapes of clouds. Maybe in Leo's imagination he had become used to seeing the old people at the community center as stately old oak trees or tall stretching old swamp cypresses.

Pittsburgh then touched Leo's eyes a second time. It was then that the old veteran saw the world as it really was. I can't explain what happened to Leo Stapelton that day. Maybe Jesus did some kind of a trick. Maybe Leo had only been pretending he was blind for all of these years, and it was this scenario that allowed him to correct that false impression. Maybe Leo was still as blind as a bat but he was now just pretending to see so that he wouldn't hurt Jesus' feelings.

Maybe Leo Stapelton was actually healed of blindness. None of us asked Jesus about it later, because, the first time we tried to get an explanation from him about this miracle he made us feel as stonewalled as a bunch of flaming gays at a Baptist social. Maybe, every once in awhile, something good happens to one of the good folks in our world. Like the old gentleman, Mr. Leo Stapelton, said, I suppose a loving and merciful God could do something amazingly great like that if He wanted to do it.

13. HIV-Positive

One day, we were walking down Malcolm X Boulevard in Harlem enroute to one of our favorite Jamaican Restaurants. Brother Jeremy stopped us along the way to introduce all of us to someone that he recognized from his NOI days. It was a sister named Big Sheena. She was wearing a Harlem Globetrotter's jacket and had wonderfully, beautiful, long braids. Under her jacket you could see a scorpion tattoo heading up the side of her body. She had a whole bunch of other "body-art" too!

At first glance, her face seemed filled with sadness. This turned out to be accurate. I found out later that doctors had informed Sheena just that week that she was dying of AIDS and that she had only had about six months left to live.

Big Sheena lightened up when she was introduced to Jesus: *"Wait, Jesus? So you are the second coming or something?"*

Pittsburgh laughed: *"Most people assume my mama and papi is Mexican and that's how I got the name. Actually, I was born on Christmas Day and my mama was a big Jesus fan; that's how I got the name. Anyway, I could've done a lot worse. Her favorite comedian was Richard Pryor and she once told me that she also almost named me after her favorite ball player – Earl Munroe!"*

Sheena smiled at the joke. Jesus had a way of putting people at ease. Then he got a little bit quieter with her. He touched Big Sheena's shoulder: *"You know what? You remind me a little bit of my mama. You're a very fine sister and obviously a very beautiful woman. I hear from Brother Jeremy that you once were a basketball player in college. From this moment on, big Sheena, you can walk away from your AIDS if you want to do that. All of the pain can be finished now. Don't tell anyone about this. Instead, find yourself a Mennonite or an Orthodox church and go inside and tell a God of love and mercy how sorry you are for any mistakes that you've made in the past. Tell Him how you intend to live your life in the future."* It seemed in that moment like a warm shine came into her eyes.

That woman told everyone that she had met about a man named Jesus who had prayed for her on the street and made her feel 100% better for the first time in a very long time. She now felt as if she was not sick at all.

Since she was so happy and was feeling better, and since she knew Brother Jeremy, Big Sheena decided to leave her shift at McDonalds and started to live and travel around with us.

Soon, everyone in Harlem's lesbian community who knew Big Sheena heard about her miracle. There was a buzz of excitement. Her friends and others who had known her in her illness saw the change and remembered how afraid she had used to be as she battled AIDS. A cloud of hopelessness now seemed lifted from her shoulders.

A community lesbian newspaper wanted to do a story about Big Sheena and Pittsburgh. Soon, one of their reporters began to follow us around. Quickly, the story went viral in the GLBT community and everyone talked about the aura and the natural energy a man who could do healings with his touch.

Some folks began to compare Jesus Scott to the energetic passion of Malcolm X, the merciful heart of Martin King, or the poetic zest of Bob Marley. Most folks, of course, dismissed wild stories about people being healed in shark tanks or coming back from the death sentence of AIDS. They argued that characters like Big Sheena were simply seeking attention from their otherwise humdrum and tragic lives. How could these healings be confirmed? Maybe these people weren't even sick in the first place.

Even if it wasn't true - it made for a great story. After Big Sheena's "miracle," Jesus wasn't able to walk the streets of Harlem without being swarmed by grateful members of the local GLBT community.

14. The Critics

Everyone wanted to touch the new-age miracle worker to get some of his magical powers. Folks wanted to take what they could from him. For every well-wisher who hoped that Pittsburgh was another reincarnation of the spirit of Malcolm X.; there were ten critics who dismissed him as another phony Father Divine, Tony Alamo, or some other kind of snake-charming charlatan. The man had the gift of making twice as many enemies as he did friends; and that never seemed to bother him in the least.

One old man claimed that when he touched Pittsburgh his baldness went away. An old geezer announced that a prayer from Pittsburgh had restored his manly virility and that he no longer needed his little blue pills. An Irishman claimed that, after he met Pittsburgh, he won $10,000 in the lottery. A grateful mother announced that Jesus had helped potty-train her recalcitrant child. You could imagine how the domino players on the streets and the preachers in the churches laughed at all of these wild stories. The smart people in town had it all figured out that Pittsburgh was a smooth con man who was stylishly working a crafty religious and new-age angle with gullible fools and the uneducated naive.

The Pastors in Harlem were the most outspoken. They noticed his name and preached that "If anyone preached of any other Jesus that I preach unto you, let that one be accursed!" This kind of frosty reception from the clergy helps explain why we usually spent our Sunday's down at Riverside or at the aquarium. Some of the saints in Harlem told us that their preachers had mockingly "invited" Jesus to come to their congregations and perform a public "miracle" as a sign that his powers came from God. Most of the Pentecostals guessed that he was working with demonic powers. The fact that the GLBT community was so much on his side was further proof of this theory. Preachers called on Jesus to simply leave town and take his travelling circus of reprobate gays and lesbians with him! Everyone knows that Bible verse that says "birds of a feather flock together." All anyone had to do was look at the company that Jesus kept to know that he was anything but a man of holiness. It was clear as day: Jesus was a single man living with a bunch of gays and queens. He was clearly part of the gay agenda bandwagon.

One of the Bishops of one of the biggest mega-churches in Harlem raised a mighty fuss when he heard that Pittsburgh had preached that some preachers were actually money-grabbing hypocrites and blatant womanizers: "*Who does this clown from the country think he is? Half the time he's hanging out in shady bars, crack houses, or strip clubs with a bunch of crack-happy hoes and lesbos. If he didn't go to so many strip clubs, I'd be certain he was gay because of all of those freaky guys that he hangs around with. This imposter thinks he can come here and fool all of us? He was born in Pittsburgh of all damned places. He's a bastard. This "Jesus", if that's even his real name; and his "miracles," are nothing more than orchestrated publicity tricks from a cheap circus magician. This dumb Negro is a disgrace to the race. He doesn't even have a GED and can't spell "C-A-T" unless you give him the "C" and the "A!"*"

The gay crowd that started flocking around Pittsburgh encouraged some of us while others of us started to become a little nervous. Before the GLBT's had started coming around Jesus like bees to honey, most folks thought of us as some secret-society gang of hoods. No one thought that anymore.

The next move from our critics was to call in the cops and say that we were disturbing the peace at all hours and were loitering and causing unspecified problems that they never really could prove. They were throwing the mud to see what would stick. Funny enough, even the friends and family members of some of our strongest critics would sometimes knock on Mrs. Palovitch's door for Jesus and ask him to pray for one of their old relatives or someone else they knew who needed a touch from God.

Honestly, I had no real problem with the haters and respected the doubts of the doubters. Their arguments were much more rational that us trying to say that God was healing people through His miraculous love and mercy. Personally, I more relate with the cynics who argue that all of humanity are merely a collection of frail bottle corks floating aimlessly on a perilous sea of suffering. Their views were more cogent than those who flocked to Jesus with their crystals and were looking for a heavenly Penn and Teller magic show. The critics are probably right that the odds are probably one hundred to one that anything miraculous can occur in the 'hood unless it comes from folks themselves who are willing to work hard and make a small, but real difference, through their own blood, sweat, toil, and tears. Maybe a psychologist could explain Pittsburgh by saying that those who touched him felt some kind of emotional release and some hope that helped them better deal with their deep pains and constant stresses. He gave them "permission" to let go of self-imposed chains that were holding them back. Maybe having a little ounce of faith is healthier than living in a stark and cold world with no faith at all. Since the poor will never have power, why not give them some bread and circuses to keep them going?

All I can tell you is that I saw some people who met Pittsburgh sick and they left him healthy. At the same time, some people go to bed healthy and wake up sick. Life seems to be pretty random. Some amazingly beautiful woman steps out to do some shopping and then her Corolla gets slammed by some guy in a hurry who is talking on his cell phone and maybe her brakes just aren't as strong as they should be to avoid an accident. Random. I cannot agree with Muslims and other folks who say that everything that happens is in the will and plan of God. If that were true, then why do the Yankees keep winning?! I think that each of us is responsible for our own lives and actions. Whatever good luck comes our way is just icing on the cake. You really know who your friends are, and what you're made of, in the dark valley.

Pittsburgh Jesus

I find it hard to buy into the fairy-tale that there's some red-skinned, pointy-tailed, devil up in a sinister observatory-belfry hidden in a cave in the mountains of Transylvania watching the street-corners of the world and scheming: "Okay, let's inflict some major suffering here;" then, boom, he presses a button and a lady's Corolla meets the front of a speeding drunk's Ford F-150. If humanity does have an ancient enemy, it's more probably that speeding stranger on the cell phone than a supernatural, jelly-boned, red devil with a pointy tail and horns. We really don't need any supernatural terrorists, anyway. We already have a boat-load of the natural ones blowing themselves up all around us. Sometimes, these devils dress like devout extremists to hijack airplanes. Other times, they dress up like holy priests and secretly molest defenseless children. Sometimes, they dress up like stock-brokers and take old folks for all of their hard-earned savings. Often, the devils around us are demagogues on Fox News Radio and politician-preachers who tell us to hate each other, especially Muzzys, in the name of Jesus and the flag.

Here's my question: was Jesus Scott ever really a "threat" to anyone? I don't think so. It may be true that some people saw him as a threat, but that was only because they had something to hide or protect. It is true that Pittsburgh did have something of a swagger about him. Maybe it was just my over-active imagination, but sometimes it seemed as if he was scanning the streets and the buildings around him as if he was on the hunt as a private detective for some mysterious murderer. His weapons were his hands and his voice and he usually was on the side of dreamers instead of realists.

Jesus spent a lot of time day and night just walking the streets and thinking. Who knows what he was doing? I'd like to imagine that he took those long walks to invent more miracles with some inner passion that helped him to see the world with different eyes and dream of how things could change.

If Pittsburgh really could heal folks with a supernatural aura like some said he could, then I wondered why he didn't empty out all of the hospitals? Why didn't he send old folks home from their miserable squalor with brand-new healthy bodies? Have you ever been to a stench-filled old-folks home? Have you ever been to a cold, god-awful hospital filled with oozing bandages, sweating fevers, paralysis, and disease? All of that is still waiting where it always was for the miracle power of a loving and merciful God. It's the fact that he never did anything like this, that leads me to guess that he never healed anybody as much as some folks were so full of faith that they healed themselves when they found some hope to add to their passion. If the world was really a place of fairness; I doubt it'd be designed like a global Chinese puzzle filled with inscrutable logarithms only accessible to the elite.

Any city in our world is chock-full of places where deaf-mutes and lunatics are locked away into institutions just waiting to die. They are full of people bobbing in a big ocean just to survive day to day with nothing to hold onto in the water but their seething inner angers and their resigned fears. Pittsburgh was not some remote idealist who pretended that the depressing corners of our worlds did not exist. At the same time, he never once was in the situation where he had to try to implore a tired nurse on her cell-phone to stop long enough to bring him a cold glass of water. Have a great day!

Some folks who came to Jesus were ready to receive a miracle while others were happy to accept the common graces of life as all the miracles that they ever hoped to receive. It is the pushy folks who try to build towers that reach the heavens or build huge boats filled with two kinds of every animal. Most folks simply take life on life's terms. Who's to say if that is good or bad? It all depends on how you look at things. The way I see it, miracles happen all the time. It is a miracle whenever you come home after a long trip. It is a miracle when you hold a hot cup of coffee in your hand in the morning and it tastes like liquid sex in a cup. While some folks wanted to make Pittsburgh out to be some miracle-working wizard, I don't think they really knew him very well. In fact, Pittsburgh may've even been an enemy of miracles if, by that you mean, the search for the extraordinary, the freak-show odd, the Ripley's-believe-it-or-not unimaginable, and the Hindu holy-man extreme. He never looked for a wizard to get him out of his own problems and never thought that he could be anybody else's personal magician bestowing free trips to heaven, perfect health, and big bank accounts. The God of love and mercy created a world full of everyday miracles. Any miracle that came from Pittsburgh was dragged from out of his pity, or salvaged like an old antique, from out of his patience, or maybe even stolen from his loving heart by the desperate cunning of somebody who was filled to the brim with seething need. What did folks come out to see when they looked for Jesus? Whatever they came for, is probably what they left with. It's true that to do a certain kind of thing you have to be a certain kind of person.

Those crowds that followed Pittsburgh waiting for a healing touch scared me. Some folks said if you touched his old jacket, or his Wiz Kids

Phils cap, you'd feel a jolt of electricity go through your body. One lady told us that's exactly what happened to her after she'd waited a few hours for Jesus to come by our favorite donut shop. She desperately plotted to steal a miracle from Jesus before he even knew what was happening. But, there was really nothing special about his Sixers jacket that I could see.

I wonder if these Pittsburgh fans and their crazy ideas terrified him as well. Maybe they are why he went away. All of the pushing and shoving native to crowds and all of the urgency of bodies jockeying to inch ahead of everyone else around them was completely antithetical to the way he liked to live his life. Everyone was imploring him and asking him for something for themselves or for somebody they knew. His days were nothing like quiet walks along the Appalachian Trail. Everyone coming up from air from long nights of being scourged and feeling alone, and looking to this stranger named Jesus to breathe on them with an eternal assurance or touch their eyes with his saliva for some magical power.

How did Pittsburgh feel walking through those crowds in cities who wanted something from him whether he could give them anything or not? If I was him, I'd have felt like I was wading through a crowded, noisy circus park on the way to face my own execution by a firing squad. That's just me.

Chapter Five:

Teachings

Like turning over a wheelbarrow

1. Nowhere Else to Go

One day Pittsburgh met an old friend that he'd known from his Harrisburg days. It was down at the Times Square TCKTs booth where they sell discounted Broadway tickets. Jesus would go there to talk with folks since most of them were out-of-towners and they had a lot of time on their hands to kill waiting in line. He also liked to talk to all of those Nigerians there selling Grey Line Tour Tickets.

The brother's name was T-Bo. He used to hang out at Jesus' grandma's house – especially around supper time. They met by accident when one of the Rock's dealers said that he had a guy working for him from Harrisburg. The Rock told his dealer that that's where Jesus had grown up. T-Bo was not all that good at the trade. He'd been in and out of the prison system since he was 14.

Trailing T-Bo was a D.E.A. officer. This guy showed up one day to question Jesus to ask him why he was hanging out with such thugs if he wasn't a dealer or a user himself. Jesus answered the agent: *"The healthy don't need doctors, Officer, but the sick could use a little healing medicine and some love. I didn't come here to lift up the righteous; they are high enough already. I'm here to love these dogs struggling for their lives and who seem to be as lost as lost as can be. Most people have lost their way home. They need a spiritual GPS to find their location. They've drifted far away from families and their roots. We can help these folks find their way home."*

That's just the way Pittsburgh was: He felt folks needed to be loved. He was always trying to make folks see what was really important in life. Charlie told us that he had a gut feeling that Jesus was leading us down the wrong track and that, sooner or later, there'd be hell to pay. Charlie ended up on the side of those in the crowd who said that Jesus was way too challenging in always confronting everybody when all folks wanted was a warm-fuzzy Oprah approach. One time Jesus asked the Rock: *"Do you want to go away too my brother?"*

But for folks like the Rock, Brother Jeremy, Rad, and myself, there was nowhere else to go: nothing to join and nothing to see and nowhere to go. We stayed because he made sense. He was a good man who could use a little help. What he said lifted people like Big Sheena or Renee up and gave them some hope. Pittsburgh wasn't really a miracle-worker as much as he was just a good friend.

2. I Never in a Million Years Wanted a Divorce

For a man who never married or had kids, Pittsburgh talked a lot about marriage and divorce. One thing he said that was really weird was that in heaven we'd not have wives or husbands but simply float around like the angels. That seemed like a real drag. He talked about how marriage was a gift from God; but so was divorce, because sometimes people's hearts would just get so hard and cold. This made a lot of sense to me because I'd been down that deserted nightmare of a long, country road.

I knew all about hard hearts. The girl I married was a real Cilantro-loving Puerto Rican named Isabella which in Spanish meant Queen or princess or something like that. She was 100% Boricua. We saw the world differently: For her, any Tuesday, and not Friday, the 13th was an unlucky day. She could dance a meringue, cumbia, or salsa without any music. She had at least thirty cousins and each of them seemed to begin every sentence shouting "Ay Bendito!"

I thought I'd live with her forever but our marriage turned into a carajo; a cafre. To be "A calzon quitao" that mamasita just didn't like me: "A mi plin! Ea rayo! Where's the rice to go with all of your meat?" Don't get me wrong, my wife was pretty and smart but that was also part of the problem. She was no Juan Bobo. Isabella knew she was brilliant; she was the center of her world and the world of her parents. She saw me as a challenge. Maybe she admired me at first; then I became a problem. She needed to be smarter than me.

I never got that memo that marriage was supposed to be a competition. I went to the market for wool and ended up getting sheared. At first I gave my all but nothing was ever good enough for her. I ran so fast my feet kept coming out of my shoes. I felt like I was trying to drive around in a broken down car and it would've been just as fast to walk as to try and to fix everything that was wrong.

Anyway, it was a weird feeling to live with a woman judging you and being upset at you all the time like you were a little kid: "When will you change? When the statue of Columbus puts his finger down! You are just mosquito larvae! Asnca en faz! Broki -You play dirty like Chicky Starr." Chicky was some old-time wrestler who her Father said always cheated.

Folks who don't want to be intimate, and prefer to be alone, on a walk, or up in some tree, shouldn't expect their pappi to change when all they really want to do is be alone and in control. I can't blame Isabella for the womanizing that I ended up doing. At the same time, it was as if I was acting out my "Cabron" role that she gave to me: "Mira canto de carbon! No te voy a dar el canto!"

Her "come-mierda" coldness killed any creativity in my heart. Did I want to cheat? Cheating was a way to ask for some unconditional love, any kind of love, from a woman who was always, and only, about conditions. The women I chased used me and I used them. It was a challenge: I told them what they wanted to hear and they told me that I wasn't a weak fool but someone with a decent heart.

Pappi used to say that if a man loves one woman he loves all women but if a man loves all women then he loves no woman. I'd known love from mami and from my sister. Once I got married, however, I lived on a performance stage constantly on audition and constantly failing. My role was to make this good woman I married unhappy, disappointed, miserable, and sad. Isabella was a health nut and hated the way I ate. She was a clean-freak and hated the way I dressed. She felt deceived. Her whole life became about changing me into the image of her Papi. Isabella didn't want me for who I was. She was happiest whenever I was gone on some long trip. My cheating gave her a way to justify her holy hatred. It was the most loving present I could give her in a roundabout way: "a get out of jail free card." In the end, she could move on with me as the sinful villain and her as the unappreciated, noble Queen.

I realize that I also changed a lot from when I first married. We grew apart and never had a love without strings even from the beginning when I had to move heaven and earth to convince Isabella that I was her best choice out of about a dozen other men who told her kind words. Maybe Isabella was one of those women who would've been a lesbian if she wasn't so religious because she sure didn't seem to like what I had to offer. The air between the two of us was as bitterly cold as thick Lake Michigan ice.

What I really needed when I met Jesus was a perspective on how love could be unconditional. Mercy was only a word in a book. Pittsburgh knew about my mess ups but never really said anything to me about my mistakes. What he did, by not exposing my mistakes, was to help me to realize that I wasn't proud of those things but also, that I wasn't healthy when I was lost on that road. My addiction for acceptance and love was as deadly as any addiction to booze or gambling. I really didn't even know what it was that I was looking for but I imagined that it was something called love when maybe it was me just being insecure and married to a woman who was also insecure and sad when the lights went off.

Sometimes, when you feel shipwrecked, you can go back and hold on to a friend that is there for you when you need some encouragement. Jesus had a way with folks that made you feel like you were not being put down or made to feel like a fool. Other folks agreed that Pittsburgh gave them a second chance to make a little more out of their lives than they were making of it before he met them.

3. The KFC

So, we stayed with him: Whether Jesus was walking around Central Park rapping for some passersby or on the hood of some Chevy at the KFC we'd stay around and listen to what he had to say about our lives of triumphs and disasters. Somewhere along the way, Pittsburgh learned the gift of storytelling. His stories reminded me of the tales my grandpa used to tell me about his dangerous travels and wars.

Sometimes, however, it was extremely difficult to understand exactly what the man was talking about. He was probably just making things up or playing games with us. He'd even ask us to tell him three things that we wanted for him to add into the story that he was going to tell. Jesus acted like the stories he was telling meant something, but, sometimes I think he was flying without either a map or a parachute. Occasionally, he'd get to the end of a story and not have any conclusion. The man never would've made any money in Hollywood.

His storytelling could go on for over an hour and I rode his rollercoaster waiting for it to ground to a halt. If I'd had a pocket knife I might've become an expert wood-carver during all of his stories. I kept my eyes on him and let his words fade into the background while I studied his face. It was enough for me to listen, because, half the time, I had no idea what he was talking about. He gathered his stories from the ghosts that he kept company with along with the birds in the trees and the rabbits in the park.

I think the man must've heard voices in his head. Other prophets, touched with epilepsy, also moved between the natural and the supernatural realms of solidness and shadow. Jesus explained that he tried to make his stories filled with things that folks understood to teach them lessons that they had yet to understand. His words made the blind see and those who saw became blind. Paradox was his gig. He kept you off guard but the darkness he took you into with his stories made sense eventually. He played words like Chick Corea played his guitar. He played; we danced. The dancing was what mattered.

4. The Times Square Church

There was an evangelical church in New York City, right in the heart of Times Square where young Christians would come to learn how to "reach the lost" with the love of the Lord Jesus Christ. All of us had big targets pinned to our backs for these kids from Canton, Ohio or Dallas, Texas to show us how they "really loved us" and didn't want us to burn in an eternal hell-fire that would burn all day until a person would fall unconscious, only to have the same thing start up all over again. Worms would also be eating out our eyes and, presumably, country and western music would also be playing all the time.

These kids "really loved us" even though they had no idea who were were or that God had always lived in our 'hood. These evangelicals called their program the *New York School of Ministry*. They'd walk around the city on intercessory prayer-walks casting out the demons that lived all over the city. They'd pass out cartoon gospel-tracts that showed little stories of people going to hell. They were some of the few folks that'd give the time of day to homeless people but the real counting coup would commence once one of the luckier ones in their number crossed paths with a Lubavitcher Jew who was just irritated enough to stop and give these naïve interlopers a piece of his Halachic mind. They would talk about the true Messiah and later gloat how they had been persecuted for the sake of righteousness. They would meet flaming gays and cheerily tell them that they could be freed from their enslavement. It was funny to me how they cast out demons from mosques or bars but never seemed to be able to find any devils over at the

IKEA or the suburban shopping malls that they flocked to every weekend. These kids knew better than we did how to live our lives even though they had no clue how to live their own. That was the beauty of going on a holy mission to reach lost souls. You had a divine mission that assumed that you weren't lost yourself. The fact that no one listened to you, or thought you were full of hot air, only confirmed how hard the hearts were of the godless pagans you were trying to reach with your lovin-spoonful. When people asked them to leave them alone; they rejoiced at their persecutions.

Sooner or later it was bound to happen: One of these suburban-born and bred zealots came up to Pittsburgh and intended to test him with a pretzel-ish theological question. It was a set-up where the answer led you right into the jaws of their cozy little world: *"Excuse me Mr. Sir. May I ask you one question? If you were to die tonight do you know where you'd spend eternity?"*

You can smell these bastards a mile away by the way they look at you with their fake pity. Their smiles are strained like old spaghetti in a bachelor pad sink. They know they have what you need: Jesus. Maybe this kid picked on Pittsburgh because the word had gotten out that some guy was going around town with a bunch of godless people talking about a God of love and mercy. More probably, it was just sheer dumb luck for Jesus; and a poor day in court for the kid from Nebraska or Illinois.

The kid hadn't even introduced himself or asked Pittsburgh for his name. Jesus said: *"Sure I know where I'm going when I die. I'm going under six feet of dirt. The problem for me is I'm not sure I know where I'm going after I get away from you! By the way, what is your name? I'm Jesus Scott."*

The kid was not about to give up. *"Jesus? Hi, Jesus – I'm Josh. Josh Zercher."* A few gay people were hugging each other a few feet away. Sodomy was an abomination and AIDS and all of the other STD's were God's vials of judgment poured out on wretched sinners. If a Christian didn't clearly attack the blatant sins of sodomy; the nation would fall like Sodom and Gomorrah into the hands of mongrel, half-bred socialists led by a smooth talking anti-Christ with a first name with six letters; a second name – when misspelled – with six letters and a last name with only one letter short of six letters. This encouraged the guy to go one step further: *"Is it lawful for a man to marry another man?"*

Jesus looked at the man almost with eyes of pity and sadness: *"What is marriage to you my brother? What does the Holy Bible say about a God of love and mercy who should love each other and be faithful and true to each other? What about divorce? Is a divorce allowed by a loving and merciful God?*

The young preacher boy thought for a moment: *"Well, a Holy God allows divorce if we get a certificate for divorce but God would never allow two gay people to get a certificate for their union."*

"Let me ask you another question then," Jesus continued, *"Isn't it true that our God of love and mercy put the laws of marriage and divorce in the Holy Bible to keep folks from abusing and hurting each other? Isn't it true that an abusive marriage of any kind is not right; but the consequences of staying in a bad marriage are even worse?*

"Most folks try to make the world a simple place of black and white and good and evil but if you were living by the fire of God's Spirit, my brother, your first thought about other folks' lives would be to ask a loving and merciful God to show you how to love them instead of judging them from the outside. Folks feel like they have no power and they slowly lose their sense of feeling; all they want to do is escape. But, a workaholic or a religious zealot is just as out of control as a crack addict. Even a crack dealer can show a little love to those who love him. Our loving and merciful God created each and every person in the world; no one should ever break down what God has created. We are fearfully and wonderfully made by our Creator. Now I have one question for you, Josh, do you know who you are and who you claim to be? Why did you pay a hooker over in Brooklyn last weekend to give you a blow job?"

Ouch! Where did that come from? It hit old Josh right smack between his Holy Bible and his WWJD bracelet. Josh zoomed off from there like a beaten stray dog with his bitten tail between his legs.

Later, I asked Pittsburgh about this. He explained: *"I tried to talk to this brother in a way that he'd understand. Instead of looking in the speck of somebody else's eye; he needed to turn his attention to the log sticking out of his own eye. A judgmental spirit will never lift up anyone. Folks who don't live in ghettoes shouldn't tell us who have to live in them how to live. God is the judge. A proud man might be farther from God than a thug filled with sin. Whenever I meet a hater; I just brush my shoulders off."*

Then he pointed to a gaggle of elementary school-children passing by. They were surrounded by three or four stressed-out chaperones: *"Look at those children: Do you think they go around judging their teachers or principles because they are gay or because they're straight? They judge their teachers based on who is kind; on who shows friendliness or thoughtfulness, or who gives them candy. Adults could learn something about the Kingdom of a loving and merciful God from these kids. They usually don't have deep biases of hatred toward others when they are little. Someone has to teach them how to act like bigots or self-righteous little princes. If you want to get to heaven, become a* little kid. Don't act like you are someone who has all the answers. Don't look down on anyone else with an attitude of scorn.

5. A Widow's Gift

From time to time folks would come up to one of us and give us a few dollars to buy a little food or to help us with bus fares. It was frustrating, however, because if folks gave any money directly to Pittsburgh he'd only have it in his hands for a millisecond before handing it off to someone else in need. He gave money to homeless beggars or mom's alone with their kids at the shopping mall. This explains why, if we guessed someone was about to give him money, we'd intervene right away. Charlie kept the money for us until it was time to buy some groceries. Charlie was the Suze Ormond in our group; he knew how to handle money. He was educated too; went to a famous school called Princeton Seminary.

One time, during the Macy's Thanksgiving Parade, we'd been watching the floats of Santa, Mighty Mouse, and Elmer Fudd going by when a homeless woman carrying a little baby on her back came up to CJ and gave him a $5 dollar bill. She asked him to give it to Jesus. That same day a few other folks had given us few $20s; one guy even gave us a Benjamin.

Pittsburgh thanked the woman for her gift. Then he told us: *"Did you ever notice how a fifty dollar bill looks so small at the grocery store and yet so huge when they are passing around the plate at church?! All of the money that folks have given to us helps out. This little sister, however, gave us the very last money that she had to buy some baby formula for her newborn. May the God of mercy bless her for her heart of generosity."*

6. Only 'Yes' or 'No'

Near the 9/11 Memorial in lower Manhattan, Pittsburgh struck up a conversation with a group of visiting tourists. A "debate" started when one of the tourists, a zealous Texan, who felt his state should secede from the Union, started talking about the need for tighter security on our borders and how rag-heads and all Muslim faggots should not even be allowed to immigrate into this great country of ours.

This fat, blonde, white guy wore a Jeff Gordon NASCAR t-shirt and tight jeans and a John Deere hat. He needed a shave and a shower. He was off on a tangent quoting some blow-hard named Lou Dobbs about how Mexicans and foreigners were turning this great country of ours into one big mixed-up, non-Anglo, brown mess. America had fallen away from its

Bible-based, slave-master, free-mason, founding heritage. He was worried that liberals were gonna take his guns away. To do that, they'd have to come down to Amarillo and pry them out of his cold, dead hands. The guy was heavy on explaining his views; but not so much on allowing others to get a word in edgewise.

Pittsburgh interrupted and took the conversation in a different direction. He challenged Tex – and everybody else listening - to think about insecurity instead of security: *"Brothers and sisters need to abandon their fear of each other and learn to follow a loving and merciful God. Folks need to stop indulging in generalized, dishonest, and deceptive stereotypes about other religions when those religions aren't even represented in our conversations about them. If they're not there; they can't speak for themselves or defend themselves. Don't you hate it when folks talk about you behind your back?*

Haters hate because that's all their good at! Haters are bitter bastards. Hate is their way to try to validate their slumlord personalities. That's why all haters end up alone and as isolated as a cat locked into a microwave. All of their relationships get smeared by their overflowing hatred. If a white man teaches his boy how to hate blacks then the boy will end up hating blacks and also everybody else.

It's okay to be angry about the World Trade Center and the horrible things that happened here on that day. But don't let your anger turn into a blind hatred. You should have zero tolerance for hatred especially at ground zero. Hatred brings us down to the level of the killers who did this and were sure that what they were doing God's will. All you're doing when you hate is raise your own blood pressure. You give the murdering bastards who want to see you die the satisfaction of your angry attention. They want to pull your chain: That is the only way that they can win. Sure, hatred gets folks energized. But it always ends up being destructive and unsympathetic. Healthy people can't afford to get dragged down into hate because they know what hate will do to them and how it doesn't ever change anything at all! Haters have morphed into crippled and deformed souls.

Even if you're trying to save your life you'll lose it if you make yourself the judge of others. The world is big. Our loving and merciful God is a big God. Folks who try to make the world as small as their own country; or, their God their own personal property, better not allow themselves to become confused by learning more, or traveling to other countries. Small folks need to reinforce their own sense of being right. They feel better knowing other folks need to become just like them if they want to get to heaven. They live in the best country in the world; even though they've never been anywhere else. They have the best religion; even though they don't even know the Four Noble Truths. They are like a man who boasts that his wife is the prettiest, his dog is the better than your dog, and his kids are smarter than your kids. They may even mean well: Folks like that probably don't realize how hard they are to deal with.

If you want to save yourself let your words be simply "yes" or "no." Hatred is destructive to both the folks being hated and the haters. Slavery and Jim Crow certainly destroyed African-American lives but they also twisted Euro-Americans into mis-aligned ghosts of immorality. We talk about al-Qaeda as terrorists; we forget that the KKK, and even some much more respectable organizations, also terrorized folks. The way out of insecurity is to love your enemies so that you'll be like your Father in Heaven. If you have ears on your head, listen to what I'm saying."

7. Tupac or a Young Barack?

Pittsburgh once asked us an odd question while we were sitting around a huge table of rice and General Tsao's one night in Chinatown. *"Who do folks say that I remind them of?"*

The Rock spoke up: *"Some say you are like David Copperfield. Others say you are like that Jim Jones guy who made all of those folks drink his poisonous Kool-Aid. Some say you are a young Barack because of your community spirit. Some say you've the same kind of stupid courage that Fannie Lou Hamer had when she didn't accept the man being in charge. Some say you are like Tupac, Marley, or Gil-Scott Heron before his drugs. That's because of how you spit commentary on how society needs to wake up and change. Most folks just think that you are homeless bum from Pittsburgh; a nobody."*

"What about y'all – who do I remind you of?" Jesus asked.

"Malcolm X without the sunglasses and the black suit and tie," the Rock answered before any of us could answer.

"Keep that a secret between us my brother, someday I'll have to get that suit and tie out of my mother's storage closet and then you'll really see me as I am," Jesus said with a laugh.

8. Fear Factor

Pittsburgh taught that fear was the seed of a weed that'd eventually take over. Fear incapacitates folks and they become helpless. They lose control of situations; then they learn to live with their fears like a cripple learns to live with her crutches. Fear is our common coping device and our safety mechanism to get through day by day without having a nervous collapse.

We even teach our children how to be afraid – to be marginalized because that's what is available to them. Just like the big daddy in the Bambi story, our Poppas tell us how not to get shot; they don't teach us how to feel any sense of freedom since they also tell us that we are being hunted.

A lot of whites live in fear. That's why they segregate themselves as far away from us brown folks as they can. They say in their words that we are equal but their actions show whom they are willing to marry, live next to, or attend church with. Segregation is more alive today in most of America when it is voluntary than when it used to be the law of the land. Some whites are afraid of learning something about us that would expose what they already believe to be true. They try to "help" us with their prayers, donations, social-working daughters, and with scholarships; but they never think that we are really equal. The stereotypes that they live with are the snow-plows that keep their brains free of snow.

We can usually come to them but don't expect many of them to come to you. How many white kids do you see even consider going to Howard or Morgan State? Bigots don't think of themselves as bigots. They're expert at massaging their own insecurities. You're a racist if you believe that there are different races of people. Jim Crow was about a few poor, white folks liking the fact that other folks couldn't eat at their lunch counters. It was about power; the need for small folks to feel like they are big. Nobodies who want to be somebodies join the army or the Klan. That's why so many poor, uneducated bastards are still in the Klan; or keep a Klan mentality. Anyone chained by fear will lead a pointless life, and will eventually die an undignified death. Their lives have no real purpose but to deal with their daily fears. A fearful man keeps himself wrapped up safe and insular: He "dies" a long time before he's dead.

Some folks live in fear all the time. Some cities have become kingdoms of mistrust. Threats are everywhere. You can be at the wrong place and at the wrong time, and you'll be beaten up, robbed, or even killed for no particular reason. A policeman can use his power as he sees fit; there's nothing you can do about it. Fear is one-sided violence. It's a toxic mood that gets into the air and then seeps all over like pollen during hay-fever season. A sister without fear breaks the power of evil. As soon as you realize you're a child of God, and not a nobody, then everything shifts in the equations of power and control.

9. Knifing the Killers

One night some of us were sitting on the stoop. Brother Cedric was in a complaining mood about what he saw going on in the city. *"Jesus, why don't we get some people to come down here and knife all these folks who are coming into our 'hood and f---- it up with their dealing? Dudes dealing on every corner are turning our sisters and little brothers into addicts and whores. Those Uncle Tom's don't even live here. Of course, they come down here and others come and buy their s----. And then our folks start selling too. Where else they gonna work? Only so many folks can flip burgers. All of us are suffering because of this s----."*

"You think I don't see that?" Pittsburgh asked. *"If we hate, we become just like our slumlords, or those white folks who come down from the 'burbs that pass out food at us. Wars bring violence and the government's war on drugs makes victims of the broken. It's not the drugs that make folks criminals – laws do that. We should be better than small-hearted souls. Love like the father loves."*

"The deceivers are weak folks who use deception against the strong. That's how the weak have always survived. Even little children, who've no real control over parents, find ways to get what they want through tricks of the trade - like crying or pouting. Some women in places where men are in control have learned how to get what they want. These dealers come into our 'hood and start out with deception. They end up filling the streets with living deceptions. Folks have no idea if they are coming or going. They've been wearing Halloween masks for so long; their masks are now glued to their faces."

10. An Overturned Wheelbarrow

Pittsburgh turned things upside down. He said poor folks were actually the richest; those of us crying now would, one day, become the last folks standing and laughing last. Listening to him sometimes made me feel like I was a little kid again on a swing-set being pushed higher and higher into the sky.

He talked a lot about healing: *""Pure hearts will know a loving and merciful God; those who've been beaten up by life will find their healing. You're actually lucky when someone insults you; using the N-word; good folks always face those kinds of insults. Watch out, however, if your college degree and your passport are your safety-net. You might only be living in a music video of your own making. You have your reward in your cars and your comforts; nothing else for you. If you're drinking the Courvoisier now, don't expect to find any of it dripping through your I-V tube when the party runs out on you."*

"Forgive others and you'll find forgiveness. Don't judge others and you'll not be judged. Help old ladies in and out of buses. Give up your seat to a lady with a baby or with a lot of shopping bags; on your last day you'll find angels helping you in and out of heaven's glory bus."

Chapter Six:

Parables

1. *"No one every spoke quite like this man"*

Pittsburgh loved Central Park. He loved to rap out some made-up stories while walking through the park with a crowd of folks following him. Then, he'd stop at some benches around a fountain and listen to the stories that the skateboarders around the park shared about their best and worst rides.

One story he made up he called the Ballad of a Brooklyn Basketball Star. It was about how the smallest kid on his local court went on to play for the Knicks and star for them. Another one he liked to tell he called the Parable of the Taxi Cabs. In that story, even though one boss owned a bunch of cabs, only a few of them were operating because of blown tires or because some were simply out of gas.

Jesus used to tell folks that our bodies were Chevy's that drove our souls around this world. We had to be careful with what God gave us and not water down our gas with weak thinking or let dirt clog the air-filters of our souls. I thought some of that talk was pretty corny. People should keep their transmission on mission and make sure and change the anointing oil of the Holy Ghost every three to four thousand miles. He told folks to keep their heart's tires from going bald. Who knows, maybe he was just saying all of that to mix in a little practical car-maintenance advice with his spiritual thoughts.

One story featured a group of dogs in a kennel in New Orleans right before Hurricane Katrina. He said that the owner of this particular kennel was able to get all of his dogs to Baton Rouge except one ugly mutt that had seemingly gone missing. While everybody else was heading north on I-10, this guy went south; back toward Jackson Square around the Café du Monde, looking for this one dog: True love. He told this story so well that you could almost see the mud on that mangy flea-ridden, scabby-faced animal and smell the sewer water that he'd been swimming in.

This story ended with the owner finding the mutt and throwing a wild, all night honky-tonk party for everyone staying at the same shelter that he and his other dogs were at. He said that party would be like heaven: *"There'll be more dancing in heaven for one repentant sister than for ninety-nine upright church-going folks. Folks need fixing up from the inside. If a proud man can't accept the truth from Barack or Oprah or Jon Stewart then how will they receive it from me? I tell you; the whores and the dealers will swim in the truth long before professors, lawyers, and preachers will be able to handle it."*

2. Grandma's Marigolds

Late on Saturday afternoon for some reason on a lark we went out to Yankee Stadium. It was the middle of the summer but the parking lot was empty because the Yanks were out of town – down in Tampa Bay. Still, there were three or four forty-somethings hanging out in the parking lot. You could smell a whole case of Jack Daniels on most of those guys.

Pittsburgh began telling them a story: *"An old grandma wanted to plant some flower seeds in front of her stoop. She was throwing them wildly so some of them fell on the sidewalk in front of her garden. The crows and birds ate them up. Other seed fell under a metal fence in front of the house. These were choked out whenever they tried to grow. Some of the seeds, however, fell on some rich, dark, garden-soil. Soon, this old mama had a bevy of beautiful marigolds. There was every color. Did you ever notice that nature flourishes wildly when left alone? Weeds, however, will eventually take a garden over if you do nothing. If you take up on your weeding and watering then what you plant will be colorful and healthy.* After we'd walked a little distance away from the Jack Daniels group he explained that. He pulled us aside and told us to be like the bright, summer flowers in that grandma's garden.

Jesus said that patches of strawberry plants were very easily overrun with weeds if you didn't stay on top of them all the time. He explained that the weeds enjoyed an unfair advantage because they had originally come from the soil while the strawberries were not native to the soil. Since they were planted with a purpose the also had to be guarded and cared for.

Strawberries in a patch were like Pentecostal Africans who have to come and live in the frigid materialism of the United States.

3. The Parable of the Welfare Check

Pittsburgh taught: "*The Kingdom of a loving and merciful God is like a welfare check you keep on receiving over and over. Even though it's a thin piece of paper – that check can solve most of your money problems for the month if you use it right. Sufficiency is planned while deficiency just happens.*"

4. The Parable of the Telemarketer

Pittsburgh told about how a telemarketer who made a living calling folks from morning to night; working on straight commission. "*When he began his work one day the first guy he called hung up as soon as he found out that he was speaking to a telemarketer. The second guy stayed on the phone and listened a little longer, but, hung up as soon as they started to talk about money. The third and fourth ladies that he called were also very rude. Both of them hung up on him pretty fast. Finally, a polite man listened to him and felt that the product the pitchman was trying to sell was right for his needs.*"

Later, Pittsburgh explained this story: "*The telemarketer is a loving and merciful God. Most folks don't even want to give Him the time of day. Some listen for awhile but hang up when there is a price that is mentioned. Finally, there are some who take the time to listen to the telemarketer and accept the offer that He has for them. What you do on the phone in private will be revealed to everyone publicly. If you respond to the offers that God makes to you He'll call you even more often but if you're rude and rebuff His attempts to reach you; He'll, sooner or later, stop calling you and leave you alone.*"

5. The Parable of the Newspapers

When Pittsburgh was a kid he used to have a modest delivery route: "*Once there was a newspaper salesman who went out early every morning to sell extra newspapers to the brothers stuck in traffic as they were coming into town. One day a sudden gust of wind blew him off balance and most of his papers went flying out of his arms. Most of the papers were lost amidst the buses and got run over by the passing cars. But a few of them were good enough to be salvaged and he went ahead and sold those copies.*"

"*Even though this brother only made a few extra dollars by going to all that work to get some of his papers back he did his job and got the word out. Those newspapers are like a loving and merciful God's eternally free message.*

Sometimes things go by the script but sometimes things happen in a way that you didn't plan. The winds of the spirit are always blowing and sometimes you have to improvise on the run and figure out what to do next based on where the winds of God are taking you."

6. The Pakistani Convenience Store Owner

Jesus called one of his stories the "Tale of the Pakistani Convenience-Store Owner": *Once upon a time there was a wealthy Republican Masonic businessman in Dallas named Bucky who was driving enroute to San Antonio for business. Since he had to travel on a Thanksgiving Day, while the Cowboys were playing the, roads were almost totally empty. Unfortunately, outside of Waco, the businessman had to suddenly swerve his Escalade to avoid hitting an armadillo in the road. He lost control and his Escalade ended up in a ditch on the side of some empty road with him being knocked unconscious."*

"Bucky had to lie there in that ditch for almost three hours. In that time, three cars pulled over to his Escalade. Only the third car, however, tried to help him. The first car was driven by the preacher of Columbus Avenue Baptist. The man had the finest credentials and was a true professional of the cloth with all of the right words. That man was able to turn a page from the phone-book into a profound spiritual lesson. That day, however, the Pastor was in a hurry to get to the Thanksgiving Reach-out- to- Care program at the church. All he had time to do was to think about calling 911. Pastor dutifully prayed for a minute or so for the man's eternal salvation from the fires of hell. Since his mind was soon full of future sermon preparations, the preacher forgot to make a call to 911.

The second passer-by who stopped was a young blonde sweet white Baylor cheerleader who'd thought about helping out the man in the car. However, when she discovered that Bucky was a man she decided to drive on in case this was actually one of those criminal tricks she'd seen on Fox TV and she decided she better get out of there before she got raped. Since it was muddy she also didn't want to get out of her car in case she'd get dirty. Anyway, she thought, she wasn't a trained professional and who knows what needs to be done. What would Daddy say? She thought – that was her lifeline and her motto. Like the preacher, she also briefly thought about calling 911 – but forgot – and also offered up a quick prayer for the man just in case he was really hurt and then she was on her way again with her Trace Adkins music as loud as ever.

After about an hour, a Pakistani Muslim convenience store owner who lived nearby saw the Escalade and immediately called the police and then called Triple A. An ambulance took the man to the hospital but the Pakistani *stayed until the car was pulled out of the ditch. The Pakistani even gave the tow-truck driver $100 and his credit card number to get the car fixed and back on the road again."*

The moral of that story might be that help will come from the most unlikely places. We have to be open to anyone and everyone lending us a hand when we are down and out. Maybe another moral of the story is not to get into any trouble on the road between Dallas and San Antonio – and especially around Waco- because you'll probably be on your own since there are not many pagans or non-church folks living down in that part of the world. Being open to God will also mean being open to other folks around us along the way.

7. The Parable of the Rent Collector

Pittsburgh told about a slumlord that went on vacation to the Hamptons. The slumlord needed to hire someone to collect the rent from his tenants while gone. He found Saif Siddiqi to collect the rent but when this man went around to some of the delinquent accounts he was beaten up because the slumlord was so unpopular. Since Saif hadn't worked out, the neighbor, still on vacation, contacted two people interested in the house. One of them didn't work out. This meant that the man, still on vacation, contacted another friend of his who knew some collectors. He asked them to help him with this particular account. Guess what? The guy got threatened with a knife.

Finally, he called on his close friend to check out the situation. When the delinquent tenant heard, after two other attempts that some bigwig was coming to collect his rent he figured that if he got rid of this guy then he'd have no further problems and could live in the place as a squatter as long as he wanted. The tenant actually threatened away the man with a gun. The next step was to call the police and they took that tenant off to jail. Jesus told this story to warn some of the police, and lawyers, and politicians, that God had their number and would deal with them once and for all if they kept putting off their duties as city officials to deal with injustices.

8. The Devil's Yard Sale

One time, the way Jesus told it, the devil was having a yard sale to try to clean out his garage of extra stuff. He put all of his tools out on the front of his lawn. He also put all kinds of different prices on the tools. Some of the most expensive tools that he was trying to sell were hatred, lust, jealousy, pride, and lying, but the most expensive tool he had for sale was a tool called discouragement.

A Brazilian guy who was working nearby stopped at the sale mainly because he was curious about what the guy in the red suit and horns with a tale might be trying to sell on his front lawn. He noticed that the tool of discouragement was the most expensive. This led him to ask Mr. Diablo to explain the higher price. *"It's like this—"* he said *"— When I can't bring down my victims with any of these other tools in my tool chest I always can rely on this one. And, one of the best things about it too, is that most folks don't even realize that it is a tool that belongs to me!"*

9. Chili Dogs at the Soup Kitchen

Another time some of his friends that he'd met on the streets told him about a soup kitchen where we could all get a good meal. The only condition was that we'd have to listen to some preacher give a long salvation sermon about how sinful we were and how we needed to have the blood of a pure and heavenly lamb poured all over our heads to wash us clean. That was a weird idea: to have lamb-blood as soap. Some preachers sure were full of themselves and seemed pretty anxious. At this soup kitchen, the preacher scanned the room as if they were salesmen in a panic to make quota. Somebody should take their blood pressure or give these guys a free vacation in Jamaica so they can unwind a little bit and not yell at folks about hell before they eat their dinner. The soup kitchen was pretty crowded the night we got there and the fact that there were an extra ten of us there didn't really help things.

The man running the shelter seemed disturbed. I didn't know what exactly it was that he was worried about. I did, however, hear Pittsburgh say to the director: *"Where's your faith, my friend? Why don't you give them something to eat?"* Jesus went into the kitchen and began to pray over the food.

Pittsburgh then told everyone to sit down at the tables. He prayed over the hot dogs, the pretzels, corn bread, Kool-aid, and the watery soup that was there that night. All of us ate and kept on eating. Somehow, there was enough for everyone. We even found some of that French Mustard and some onions and chili for our dogs. Instead of running out of food, there were even leftovers, about ten grocery bags full, that were saved for the next night.

Those were some of the best chili dogs I've ever had even though the folks who ran the Mission swear they never had any onions or chili available for that dinner that night. I think they might've really had all of that food stashed away somewhere for some special occasion. I think the encounter with Jesus, however, made them open up and get out the food that they were hoarding.

One brother speculated that what had happened was that one of the supply trucks for the month had arrived just as the dinner was being prepared. They then donated some extra food that they didn't need. I'm not sure if those dogs were made in a factory or right then and there out of thin air. However it happened, the meal was delicious and there were plenty of leftovers for the next time.

Chapter Seven:
Human Encounters

"My pleasure is to be with the sons of men."

1. Connecticut

When Pittsburgh was walking through Times Square he was jostled by a wealthy stock-broker type who was probably from some quiet suburb in Connecticut so I'll call him 'Connecticut.' He was probably a slum lord on the side; investing his spare thousands in 'hoods he'd never see from street-level. He sneered at us if we were down-on-our luck, dirty tramps. The man oozed with healthy, young, and strong ambition: spit and polish. He had the kind of face you see on billboards all over Manhattan.

Connecticut was from a crowd that'd either already made it in the world or were already well on their way. Nothing else mattered but making as much money as was possible: Roth IRA's, liquidity, and an investment portfolio were their 'Father, Son, and Holy Ghost.' These types were way out of our lives except that we vaguely knew that they lived in obscene comfort; with huge aquariums filled with octopi in their bathrooms. Their wives and daughters were the same folks who came down from their churches to give out food, pick up trash, or 'touch' our souls through their middle-men; the inner-city ministries.

Pittsburgh was doing some street preaching in the park when he ran into Connecticut. Jesus was talking about living forever; this must've caught the man's attention. Connecticut came up to that poor black man and asked an odd question: *"You seem like a good guy. Tell me, how I can gain eternal life?"*

It seemed that Connecticut was weeping; maybe he just had hay-fever. Jesus looked at him: *"Why are you calling me good, my friend? It is our loving and merciful God alone is good?"*

"You're obviously very religious - an Episcopalian or a Presbyterian right? – You probably know all about playing the God-game. There is one thing, however, that you need to do to reach God. Go this afternoon to the slum-house that you own down in Stuyvesant and give $10,000 to the janitor who lives in 6D of the East Bay Apartments. His name is James Kler Jones. You can't miss the brother's door- it is the only one in the entire complex with a kick-ass Pittsburgh Steelers sticker on the door. Then find an ATM, take out the max allowable; then, along with all the money in your wallet spread some Benjamins all over Stuyvesant – give them out to every person you meet on the street.

This is your path to mad riches in heaven one day: Sell your house in Old Saybrook and give the money to the American Indian College Fund or to scholarships at Spellman; donate your timeshare in Florida to the Gainesville Catholic Worker House; give your new Lexus away to the Quakers and, then, after a few months of some extremely intense remorse, you'll probably become a truly happy brother!"

Connecticut walked away: Too much to ask. Pittsburgh turned to us: *"Don't playa hate! Be thankful you don't have to make the same kind of decisions that brother has to make because you're already pretty much poorer than a lost, mangy, beat-up dog living under a bridge to keep out of the rain.*

How hard is it for a fat cat with crazy loot to buy a ticket to heaven? It's easier for Big Mama to become anorexic! It's easier to fly a 747 safely through the Holland Tunnel without a scratch than for a rich man to follow a loving and merciful God with all of their hearts, and without any pre-conditions."

"Is there any hope for that rich man?" I wondered out loud.

"Probably not." Jesus said laughing. *"No. Seriously, with a loving and merciful God – anything is possible."* For Pittsburgh, it was as if the simplest things were the hardest and the hardest things were the simplest. The basic

question was: can a rich American get there from here? If you want to travel north, maybe your GPS will send you south for awhile. Usually, however, the most direct route is best.

Pittsburgh said folks should be measured, cool, and stay away from what he called *the spiral*. Some folks start out okay when they're little kids selling lemonade for a quarter but end up as a mess caught up in deep dung piles of credit card debt. When they were kids; their parents made sure that they had their immunization shots to stay healthy. Now, nobody was checking up on them. A lot of folks needed a spiritual booster shot to keep them from slowly dying of AMFV- the American money flu virus.

Visit any American bookstore: What's one of the biggest sections of books? It's the "self-help" section. It's as if all these folks who are trying to add an inch to their height, or who are struggling by buying one self-improvement book after the other, are trying to dig themselves out of the grave-pits that they are digging for themselves through the love of money. Folks who want to get healthy in their souls need to slow down and take control of their lives and not live as if they were playing a video game.

Folks seem to be filling up their world with a Niagara of words, words, and more words. Pretty soon they're drowning in a sea of theories, ideas, and concepts that only mess with their heads. Happiness is not "out-there" somewhere else; it's right at home with our friends, family, and community. Our treasure is not under some old pyramid in Egypt; it's right under our noses! Folks are way too busy. In the Roman Empire, people went to the Coliseum for entertainment. In America, the "Coliseum" is a TV and computer screen which keeps them distracted in their homes. At the same time, they're always complaining about being tired while they rush around trying to make their day-to-day as complicated as possible: They've got more urgent, must-do things on their schedule than flavor that Beyonce's got in her hips and lips combined. Time to slow down and chill.

Some folks are as fake as a three-dollar bill. They end up with fake solutions to real problems. Pittsburgh said folks needed to find balance from intensity-religion or political-anger. Neither Rush Limbaugh nor Creflo Dollar was really helping anyone except their own pocket-books. Nobody has God's personal cell-phone number. Some folks are making a U-tube cartoon out of the story of their lives; caught up in stuff that really doesn't matter. They may feel patriotic, or religious, but they're just like the little guy behind the curtain in the Wizard of Oz; all hat and no cattle. The way of a loving and merciful God goes through the wilderness and through long hours caring for folks enroute to the Big Kahuna. If you're all about East Coast and Tupac just be yourself; and why not love the West Coast and Biggie too.

2. A $50 Bass Pro Shop Gift Certificate

Pittsburgh hung out with all kinds of different folks from every imaginable walk of life. One time, he left us for a few days while we were in D. C. to go over to Hagerstown, Maryland. He went to meet with a prominent businessman, outspoken gun-rights activist, and a blatant racist named Edward Nathan Declan. Mr. Declan was probably also a Klansman. When he asked to meet Jesus after reading about him in some newspaper, we all worried that Pittsburgh might be being set up to be murdered.

Pittsburgh said that he showed up at Declan's mansion for dinner with about ten white businessmen: pheasant and turtle soup. Declan asked dozens of leading questions about religion and politics: Obama and Jesus. He asked, for example, if folks should pay taxes to support the war in Afghanistan since Pittsburgh criticized the government for spending so much on the military. He answered this question with a question: *"Whose faces are on the one and two dollar bills and whose face is on the twenty?"*

Mr. Declan answered: *"George Washington, Thomas Jefferson, and General Andy Jackson."*

"Exactly!" Jesus said: *"Slaves should give to the slave master what he requires; the children of a loving and merciful God should give to God what God requires. If you give even one dollar to a homeless lady, or to a Pakistani immigrant family, it's as if you're giving that dollar directly to our merciful God."*

Pittsburgh used this dinner to tell those ten businessmen to stop charging more at their inner-city outlets than they did in their suburban stores. He told them to close down their check-cashing stores and to start putting a few bank branches inside the city limits. They listened with amusement.

After dessert, Declan sent Pittsburgh on his way with $50 for a taxi back to the city and, also, for some unknown reason, a $50 gift certificate at a Bass Pro Shop. Pittsburgh never used it. It was found on his smashed-up corpse when he was killed in 2009; it was one of the ways that they identified his body.

3. An Orthodox Priest

One time Pittsburgh met an old Greek, or Armenian, Orthodox Priest from D.C.; Father Nicholas Michael Kainaroi. The Father had a long, rough, grey beard and he wore black clothes and a dog collar. Father Nick wasn't the thinnest guy either – a few donuts in the basket if you know what I mean. The two men met after Jesus was contacted by a friend of the priest and told that Father Nick had some questions and was hoping to talk with him privately. The priest's friend asked Jesus if he'd be willing to visit with Father Nick at 6PM that same night at the Howard University-area Holiday Inn, room #228.

It was another odd request but Pittsburgh took it in stride.

Father Nick wasn't sure exactly who this Jesus was, or what he stood for. Those of us who knew Pittsburgh over time were empowered by his friendship and mystified by his comforting words. Jesus had helped us in the same way that a tree-pruner might help a home-owner by removing some old, dead branches that were blocking the view of the sun. For example, I was on much better speaking terms with despair than hopefulness before I met Jesus. For other folks, however, a poor black man with a confrontative style about the sins of the white community was not really someone that they were interested in meeting. Jesus made some folks angry while others found him a source of encouragement.

Father Nick unlatched the door and welcomed Pittsburgh to his hotel room at the Holiday Inn. He offered him a Coke or Diet Coke from the mini-bar. Inside of a minute, the priest had launched into his eager question: *"How is it possible to touch people like you do and touch God Almighty like you do?"*

Pittsburgh laughed: *"You're a great preacher and, yet, you're asking this to ME? Okay: Unless you're a classical musician who knows by heart the lyrics of both Tupac and Biggie you cannot enter the Kingdom of a loving and merciful God. Unless you as a white brother can recite for St. Peter at the gates every one of the principles of Kwanzaa; he isn't going to get in; and, he won't let in a black brother unless he can answer the test question of what major league picture in baseball history won the most games."*

"That's an easy question: Y is for Young – The Magnificent Cy; People batted against him but I never knew why! The answer is - Denton True "Cy" Young; Cleveland, St. Louis, and Boston: 511 wins."

"Cy Young was easy for you; but your question is on the seven principles of Kwanzaa. So, start by getting your Kujichagulia on and a loving and merciful God will take over from there." God is like the wind; if you want to follow a

loving and merciful God, you've gotta flow like the wind. When He moves you move- just like that – when He steps you step – just like that. If you're not following me when I'm talkin' baseball – how do you expect to stay up with me talkin' about the Seven Principles of Kwanzaa?"

"I don't get it but I think I've heard enough: Good night, Mr. Scott and thanks for being willing to coming over here to meet me. Guess you better go now. We both probably have other things to do."

"Take it easy Father Nick. Try to read some James Baldwin novels if you get a chance. Nice to meet you: Sleep well. Umoja! Imani! Nia! Ujamaa! and Kujichagulia to get you started on the way!"

4. An Illegal African Muslim Immigrant

One morning, in Battery Park, New York City, Pittsburgh met an African Muslim woman wearing a long black *hijab*. She asked him for some help while he was at the part of the park next to the boat docks where the tours leave for the Statue of Liberty. The place was crawling with foreigners and tourists. Some of them listened into the strange conversation going on between Pittsburgh and this woman.

I'll call this African Muslim, Javad. She'd heard about how Jesus had used a Hebrew blessing to take away cancer from the daughter of Howard Kenig, the deli owner. She asked him if he'd pray a blessing for her seventeen-year old daughter in Arabic. The daughter was sick with sickle-cell anemia.

Instead of answering Javad's "Salaam Aleykum" for an Arabic blessing; Jesus began to publicly confront her about her immigration status right there and then in front of all of those lines of tourists.

I'd never seen him relate to anyone in such a rude way before. Javad was honest: She answered that she was an illegal immigrant who'd overstayed her student visa. She explained she didn't think she could get good medical care for her daughter's illness in her small, ramshackle village in eastern Mali.

Jesus continued to be rude and very loud to her: "*Look little Miss rag-head piggy! You're a Muslim terrorist pig-girl; and I'm an American Christian man born and bred in the red-white-and blue. I don't worship no moon god or follow a pedophile epileptic! The fact is you're an illegal Muzzie criminal in this great country! I should report your little rag-head to the police right now. Get outta here!*"

Something was going on between the two of them. She blinked at him and smiled: "*Yes, you're totally right, Uncle Sam. I'm just a poor, little

Muslim Miss Piggy in your great, big, beautiful country. But, isn't there even one American mud-hole where an ugly, smelly, pig like me could wallow around?"

Pittsburgh started to laugh. *"That was good my dear sister! Waleykum Salaam! Go home and you'll find that your daughter is healed of her disease."*

Then he turned to the crowd and shouted: *"I've been to a lot of churches in a lot of cities in this country but I've never met an America-born Christian with the amount of persistent faith that this dear African Muslim woman has just shown. Carelessness is the great avenger. Listen! Never call unworthy the son or daughter of a loving and merciful God. If you want to be number one; then sometimes you have to be the last. If you want to sit at the front of the bus; then sometimes you have to take your seat at the back and wait for the driver to call you to the front. Oh, and one other thing: wherever you sit on a public bus – please remember to keep your feet off the seats – that's just common-sense courtesy."*

5. A Little Honey

The folks who lived around the Hallelujah AME Zion Church in Brushwick, Brooklyn, had gotten tired of walking past a local prostitute working a corner in front of the church. Pastor Hoffman contacted the owners of a few local businesses and circulated a petition that the cops should take this hooker to jail. The cops showed up at the start of the next Wednesday Night Bible Study and arrested the lady.

The minute Pittsburgh heard about this he went looking for a cab – something he never did – and hurried down to the precinct jail to pay her bail. God knows where he got the money for that bail from. When he met her, the first thing he did was confirm that Angela Benson, and not "Caramel" was her real name. The next thing he did was to take the woman back in a taxi up to the Hallelujah A.M.E.

It was about 9:30PM and the Jesus took Angela by the arm and went right into Pastor Hoffman's office. The Pastor stood up shocked: *"What is the meaning of this? If you knew who I was, and who this woman was, you wouldn't be here right now! Should I call the cops or should I call your mama, Angela?"*

Pittsburgh saw a notepad on the Pastor's desk and picked it up and began to write a name slowly and carefully. He showed it to Hoffman. Who knew who "Temeka Miller" was, but her name on that pad drew a dramatic and instant response from Hoffman. Pittsburgh then told the

Pastor, never to threaten his daughter again unless he wanted it publicly-known that he'd once paid for the services of a lady for the night. Needless to say, that was the last time that Angela Hoffman Benson, had any trouble with her neighbors, the church, or with her Daddy.

It's often a short step between sex and death, or sex and prison. This woman and that preacher too, tried to live close to the edge of the cliff of lustful hunger. You've read in books where so many ladies stab their lovers in the darkness after lovemaking like black-widow spiders or you watch movies where a John will kill a hooker right after paying for her tricks. Men and women have plenty of stones in their hands to throw at each other if things go wrong. A lot of times, those stones are hard words and smug faces. A lot of folks -too many to count -eat and drink a lot of false hopes when they're alone with each other. Jesus stepped right into the middle of this minefield when he tried to help Angela Benson.

It'd been a long day of too much drama and not much sleep for the woman. Pittsburgh invited Angela to a local Mediterranean Grill for some coffee and a delicious, mouth watering *shwarma*. Then he gave her the best gift he had to give; greater than paying the bail for her or confronting her father for her. He sat down and listened to her talk. One hour, two hours, and three hours: She told her story of a daddy's girl and about her broken dreams and lost hopes. He just listened.

It was a 24-hour Greek place so nobody was hurrying them. People came and went. The kind waitresses kept refilling their coffee cups. You could hear the pots and pans being washed in the kitchen. Angela shared her heart and showed Pittsburgh her frail heartbeat. After hours of that coffee, that woman never went back to her street-corner life again. She moved far away from her past out to Portland, Oregon, and, the last time I'd heard she was working in an art gallery as an event-receptionist.

Pittsburgh loved women. His relationships with them were mixed and varied. He loved to be with saintly old mothers, tired soccer moms, tired prostitutes, or bouncy little girls at the church nursery. You could tell that women in general had some kind of magical effect on him although he tried his best not to let them know that. He was a woman in a man's body. He loved the musical sounds and symphonies of their strong or weak voices. He loved their touch on his shoulder or on his arm or when they gave him a hug. He loved to listen to them ramble about some harmless preoccupation. The sound of a woman's voice telling her story was like the taste of sweet honey to the heart of Jesus.

All of his life, he'd been surrounded by mothers and sisters. He had smelt their perfume and watched them laugh and cry. All of his life, the bastards who tried to put him down were usually self-righteous, fat, white men wearing suits and ties. Pittsburgh never took a "vacation" per se. Instead, when he needed a break he'd go for a coffee and strike up a conversation with any lady who happened to be there about her kids or her grandkids or about the stories of her life; the honey of her heart.

6. Chucky Cheese

Jesus loved Chucky Cheese's and joked that, if the Buddhists were right about reincarnation, that, in his next life he'd work as a clown living off of tips in one of their franchises. I despised "eating" at these vortexes of pure bedlam; the constant noise invariably gave me a splitting headache. The place was a veritable laboratory of runny noses, armor-piercing screams, and shrill demands for more pieces of pepperoni. Thank God for an IPod or a walkman to plug into your ears at places like this: While, all around, kids were shouting dumb, corporate ditties; a brother could escape into some old school Chaka Khan, smooth Charlie Parker, bright reggaton Daddy Yankee, or even sweet Rasheeda offering me to take her "to yo mama's house." A Chucky Cheese was really the best place in the world to settle the debate, once and for all, about which worked the fastest or the strongest -- Tylenol, Motrin, or Advil.

Pittsburgh loved the place because he loved to be around little kids. He felt sorry that they'd eventually have to grow up and start fighting Democrats if they became Republicans or vice versa. As long as they were running around from one token-eating, noisy monster to the other there was no room for xenophobia, racism, sexism, bigotry, yada-yada.... Kids just want to play. Looking at those little kids it was hard to recognize which one would later become a junk-bond trader, a hard-hearted slumlord, or a sleazy shift manager at K-Mart who wouldn't allow folks to skip the night-shift to attend somebody's birthday party. I guess all of that devolves into the hearts of folks later over time.

Come to think of it, Pittsburgh had a little bit of a kid in him. I doubt it was the horrible food that brought him to this hellish den of dining iniquity. Maybe, right before folks rise to heaven or fall into hell, they call out for their mamas and remember playgrounds and places like Chucky Cheese that they had fun at while they were kids. Watching kids run around a pizza place, it was sad to imagine that some of them had already been abused, fondled, raped, or terrified by preachers who promised that they'd surely burn in a lake of hell-fire if they didn't immediately give their five-year old hearts to Jesus Christ.

I remember a kid once coming up to Jesus and asking him if he had any extra coupons or game tokens. That was really all that was necessary for peace and happiness in the Chucky Cheese-world. Jesus was broke as usual but Rad had one or two in his pocket; he handed them off to the little beggar.

Pittsburgh said: *"Thanks for that Rad — it'd be better for the bastards who messed with these little kids for a ball and chain to be tied around their necks and for them to be dropped into the middle of the Atlantic than for God to get a hold of them. Little kids can also show us how to pray to a loving and a merciful God. Follow their lead and pray like this- Our Father, the door is open for you to come in. We see you all around. Keep us from scorpions, jellyfish, and the folks who charge too much for second-hand batteries or tires. Give us enough pizza to eat and enough money to pay for the pizza. For you are the music and you are the music maker; keep us singing and keep us dancing. Amen, Amen, and Amen."*

Chapter Eight:
The City

1. *"And then Cain Built a City"*

Pittsburgh was a city person. He loved walking the streets late at night and talking with folks. Cities were a place of pilgrimage for him because he loved to explore the potential and possibility of each distinct place. The hustle and bustle empowered him. There is a hatchet in the hand of most cities that is able to cut away fakeness and contrivance. A song may go on for awhile but eventually you'll have to pay the piper. There wasn't much mercy for posers. The folks who claimed to love a city, but only in the same way that a person loves a playboy pin-up like Liv Lindeland, would be exposed sooner or later.

Every place had its share of horrific rapes, robberies, and murders; but most of these were focused on by folks who lived in the suburbs. If class-warfare ever broke out in America it was pretty clear whose side the devil and whose side God would be on. Satan had houses in both the city and the suburbs. But, did you notice how busy a city gets around five o'clock when everyone is trying to abandon it? The good news was that the wind of the Holy Spirit was the wind that blew through the windy city and the light of the world was who kept people awake in the city that never sleeps.

Pittsburgh had been living in New York since his run in with the police but, in January 2009, he decided he wanted to move back to D. C. The plan was also for Mama Shenice to move down from Harrisburg and join us. We wanted to fly under the radar-screen and move back to a different part of D. C. The word got out, however, that Pittsburgh was coming back. We discovered that some folks, we didn't actually know who they were, were waiting for us when our bus pulled into the Baltimore Greyhound station. They had some hand-made signs and, even though it was freezing outside, some of them took off their coats and began waving them at our bus. Folks were shouting out the name of Jesus. The vast majority of people at the station, however, had no idea what was going on with us. Most folks were focused on the sadness of the recent Ravens playoff loss or the excitement of the upcoming Obama Inauguration. Jesus was focused on neither. I heard him mutter something strange: *"What do I have to give you, Baltimore? I was hoping to bring you something the same way a mama pigeon returns with food for her baby chicks."* While the suits in a tourist office pretend their city is a mirage; what is really being cooked up on the streets is a thick stew. Real places for real people; asphalt planted in sweat.

Down in the gutters of a city the king rat was the one that was the most aggressive. Roaches and rats hold more power than politicians or preachers. Cities easily make enemies because they cannot be controlled and they are too messy for those who mouth-off about the glories of a clean, organized ideal. It was down in the cracks, according to the great prophet Tupac, where the life of any city is lived.

2. Ice on the Interstate

We were supposed to leave for D.C. at midnight but the bus didn't leave Baltimore until after 4AM. The whole time we waited the weather just kept getting worse. Traffic was also heavier than usual for that time of day because folks were coming into town for the Inauguration. The snow kept falling and, soon I-95 had become a sheer sheet of ice. Our Greyhound slowed to a crawl. Every few feet became an accomplishment. It was the worst storm I could remember and, the fact that our bus driver was swerving all over the place only added to the stress. His driving made me feel like I was in a winter-version remake of the movie *Speed*. I've never been on a plane but I guessed this is how it felt when they hit one of those jet streams and started to drop into the ocean. It seemed like we were just about to hit every car that we passed. Why in the world was our bus driver trying to pass folks anyway?

Can you relate to my terror? Death is something ugly when it is shoved into your face. Amazingly, Pittsburgh was sleeping like a baby in the middle of this driving snow-storm. I couldn't imagine in a million years how anyone would be able to sleep. For me, the storm had moved from the highway right into my heart. I was certain I was going to die and I wasn't the only one: JF was sitting next to Pittsburgh. He shoved him in the ribs with his elbow to wake him up:*"Don't you even care that we're about to get into an accident?"* The exact moment that JF woke up Jesus, the storm stopped. The sky was as calm as could be in a New York second. Just sayin'....

3. Arrival at the Greyhound Station

When we got to the city at around 8AM, there were some folks waiting to meet us. The cops had heard we were coming and they were out in force at the station. They'd even set up barricades. The folks who were waiting for Pittsburgh, however, were so happy to see him that, when he got off the bus, they just jumped over the barricades; the cops did nothing to stop them. Some of these folks were relatives of those Pittsburgh had healed. When he came off the bus a few of these kind folks spread some newspaper under his feet as a way of making sure that he didn't slip on the ice.

One lady threw some rose-petals which fell on the shoulders of Pittsburgh. Where in the world did she get roses in the middle of winter? Everyone was shouting. Maybe the carnival in Rio has the same vibe; but I guess that goes on for three-days non-stop while folks hit the streets to do the Samba.

The shouts of the crowd seemed as if they were mechanical and piped in over a sound system. The place sounded like a Chucky Cheese for adults. I couldn't tell if it was a lynch-mob or one of those crowds that a South American dictator pays to valorize his autocracy. Some folks hoped that Jesus would become their own personal king of favors. They requested miracles the same way a guy would request a radio D.J. to play an old love song. These were the same folks who'd cheer against Donovan McNabb when he was a hated Eagle and, for him when he became the quarterback for their beloved Redskins.

One shouter claimed that Pittsburgh had been responsible for miraculously healing him after a motorcycle accident. He was shouting out: *"You're the King! You're the Man! Come by my house for all of the beer and bratwurst that you want! Aint none better than the J-man Scott! J-E-S-U-S!"*

There were also reporters waiting at the station to ask a few questions: *"Mr. Scott- Did you flee D.C. before because of the rumors of the murder that you were accused of committing? Did you do it? Did you see the murderer? Was the person who killed the man one of your friends? Was he an enemy?"*

Pittsburgh kept walking forward; the crowd opened up like the Red Sea. He was cutting through the crowd like a knife through hot butter. It was almost as if he could turn an entire crowd into a group of his friends in the same way that the Lord Jesus Christ in the Holy Bible could turn water into wine.

Because the press of the crowd was so strong the Rock had the idea of commandeering a taxi at knife-point and told the driver – *"I need your wheels – Jesus needs them."* Since there were so many cops around this was a massively bad idea. Fortunately for the Rock, there was so much confusion and, soon, there was also no longer any need for a taxi. Pittsburgh had walked out of the station and had just kept going. Before anyone really noticed his crime, the Rock had put his knife away and returned the keys back to the bewildered taxi driver. He then tried to run after Jesus and the rest of us.

4. One Angry Brother

We moved into our new apartment and most of us decided to spend the rest of the day sleeping. At around 4:30, however, Pittsburgh decided to go out and take a look at our new surroundings. It was late afternoon and it was starting to get a little dark. We were used to Jesus talking to himself and he was doing it again this afternoon. As he was walking he looked up to the sky and simply said to no one in particular: *"Do I really have to do this?"*

We had no idea what he was talking about. After a few blocks, we came to a large street-market. The place was buzzing; folks were selling knock-off jewelry, watches, sunglasses, and name-brand t-shirts. Pittsburgh stopped. What made him angry was the fact that all of the trinkets for sale were exorbitantly priced and of a very poor quality. The customers didn't have much money to begin with before they fed these greedy folks with their last dollars. Poverty seemed to create more poverty. Jesus explained: *"There'll always be section 8 housing, food stamps, and folks betting on dog fights."*

A storm inside of Pittsburgh blew up and erupted like a volcano. Maybe it'd been the stress of the long bus-trip through the night. Maybe he just needed some sleep. Anyway, watching these folks get sucker-punched really ate at his gut. All of a sudden, Jesus rushed to the entrance and started to knock over the sales booths.

Sunglasses and trinkets went flying everywhere. Pittsburgh stood in the middle of the market shouting at the top of his lungs: *"Our people need decent markets where fair prices are on decent products. You felons are exploiting this community and turning this market into a crack-house"* The cops came soon after Jesus left. They decided, however, not to follow-up and seek his arrest just yet.

5. Walking on the Potomac

When we got back to our apartment, the landlord had been told about what happened at the market. Jesus was persona non grata. Since we'd not yet signed a lease he told us that he'd no longer rent his place to us. He didn't want any trouble.

It was about seven o'clock when we found this out. It was also cold and we realized we had no place to go on short notice. The landlord did have mercy on Mama Shenice, since she was an old lady. He arranged for her to stay at the parsonage of the local Catholic priest who had a spare bedroom. The rest of us, however, were - literally - out in the cold. We walked to the Potomac and went to the bridge below Georgetown as our shelter until we could make other arrangements. Tomorrow would be better.

Around midnight, we made a fire under the bridge and fell asleep. Early in the morning, when I woke up, Jesus was nowhere to be found. Sure enough, he was about sixty yards away from the rest of us out in the middle of the river. He'd made his way out on some ice, but I had no idea what he was doing.

The ice didn't seem very thick but Pittsburgh looked like he was in the middle of the river. When the Rock saw where Jesus was, he decided on a whim to go out and see what he was doing. The Rock was as crazy as a transvestite hooker. He had a stupid sense of courage, but, at least he tried things while most folks would just stay on the sidelines. If you told him to jump off a bridge he'd probably try it without taking the time to strap on his bungee cord. I doubted the man would live to see his hundredth birthday. It can be a razor-thin line, sometimes, between bold faith or courage and absolute stupidity.

Maybe the Rock was too heavy. He got out about fifty yards and then fell right through the ice. Fortunately, Pittsburgh saw this and was close enough to run over and fish him out of the icy river. From where we were on the shore, both of our friends looked like ghosts out in the middle of the river. The two of them took their time coming back over the ice to the shore and we made a quick fire right then in the hopes that the Rock would not die of exposure or pneumonia from his arctic mis-adventure.

Chapter Nine:

The Passion

"He began to be afraid and sorrowful."

1. A Bottle of Liz Taylor's Perfume

Just a few months after Obama was sworn in as our first black president, things began to unwind very quickly. Everything got tighter in the city and everyone seemed tense and on alert. The D. C. police had our number but it even seemed like the Federals might also be following us around. You know what they say – "just because you're paranoid doesn't mean they are not following you." It could've been stress.

The cops will always be the cops and the powerful have a way of assuming the worst about the powerless. We felt like a hungry lion was at the door. The cops acted like they thought that Pittsburgh was up to something and they started to let their suspicions take root. One of them told us they would probably call him in again for further questioning about the earlier, unsolved murder case.

Meanwhile, we found a decent apartment off of New York Avenue and near to the Gallaudet School for the Blind. In a nearby park some Haitians and Jamaicans put together a "Winter Carnival Festival" and we decided to check it out. While we were there, Pittsburgh said mysteriously: "*The time is coming soon"* – and suggested that Mama Shenice and everyone set up a big feast for the following day.

We agreed on a time and a place; the community hall in Dr. Tait's Faith Bible Church. As we were sitting down to eat, Renee came with a huge bottle of Liz Taylor's White Pearls -expensive perfume- and poured it over Pittsburgh's head. The stuff gooped up in his hair, ran down his beard, and made a mess all over his jeans and jacket. She was crying and was brushing her hair on his wet shoulder.

The wonderful smell of that perfume filled the hall. I couldn't believe that she'd poured out so much perfume because it was such a huge expense and I knew she wasn't a rich woman. I bought just a tiny bottle for my ex- once and it really set me back a piece of change. I had no idea why Renee did that.

For some reason, this act made Charlie laugh; he ran out of the hall. Jesus watched him go out and shouted after him: *"Do what you have to do quickly."* Then, sensing we were surprised by what Renee had done he explained: *"Don't bother Sister Renee. This is her way of getting me ready. Soon, some white folks will arrest me. What the Sister has done for me was a beautiful thing. Decades from now you'll tell your grandkids about what she did because, tonight, I'm about to go away from you."*

We continued to eat. Nobody knew what to say. I wondered where he was going and how long he'd be gone. The dinner wasn't fancy and there really wasn't much. I bought a few bags of chips. Big Sheena had some extra money from her welfare check so she went down to the wine store and came back with three good bottles of wine. Mama cooked up some of her famous biscuits.

Jesus took some of Mama's biscuits and broke them and began passing them around. Mama Shenice encouraged us: *"Do whatever he tells you to do. His hour is coming."* Maybe he was thinking out loud, but he started to say some things that were pretty strange: *"I've been looking forward to this meal with you. This is bread is like my broken body."* He asked all of us to all take a piece of a biscuit. Then he took some wine: *"This wine is like my blood which will soon be spilled."*

He then said, *"One of you will help get me killed!"* The whole scene reminded me of the Jim Jones thing at Jonestown where they all took the Kool-Aid and died; or the painting in the DaVinci Code where Christ sits with His followers. I must say Mama Shenice's biscuits are the best I've ever eaten.

The Rock didn't like the drama: *"Don't talk about death – Jesus; we won't let anyone touch you. None of us would ever hurt you,"* None of us could imagine how one of our friends could play a hand in betraying him. Then again, that's what happened to Tupac, Biggie, and Malcolm; that's how a good brother sometimes meets his end. Violence seems to be everywhere like a pack of wild wolves.

Pittsburgh looked over to the Rock at the end of the table: *"Guaranteed- before you hear a police siren sound three times, you'll be as gone, as gone can be. You'll be telling white folks that you don't even know me. But, don't worry, even if you tear down all of the projects in D. C. – God will rebuild them in three days."* Rock looked stunned: *"No way! I'm your main man. I got your back."*

Then Pittsburgh started out with a shoe-shine kit to shine all of our shoes. This was jazz at the improv to the max. He was going to work in the same way that a dog would come under your table and start chewing on some bones that somebody had snuck under the table. It took him about an hour but he cleaned everybody's dirty sneakers. I had the nicest pair – MJ 360's – but they actually did need some spit and polish to shine them up. Maybe the man just liked clean shoes.

One thing about Pittsburgh, he never needed your pity. He never even wanted our gratitude. All he ever wanted was that we'd stay with him. Everybody's days are numbered; my grandma told me once that some folks know exactly how many days they have. Some folks can even chose the hour that they go. That's what happened to my father when he was dying of cancer. The doctor gave him six months to live but dad was stubborn; he starved himself to death inside of a week.

2. One of Us

After midnight, on April 4, asleep on the sofas in the apartment where we were staying, Jesus woke us up and said we needed to go down, right then, to DuPont Circle.

We had no idea what was going on. The streets were dim. Trash blew in the wind, and along the sidewalks, and into the gutters. It was cold. There was a dusting of crusty snow on the ground.

Because Pittsburgh had been talking so much about death, the Rock was nervous. He was the only one that was packing. While we were walking I saw him come alongside Jesus and hand him is Glock. As soon as it was in his hands, Jesus wheeled around and threw it into a dumpster: *"The weapons we're using are stronger than what you gave me. Use your heart and this"* he said pointing to his head. I really don't think the Rock appreciated Pittsburgh throwing his $300 piece into the trash.

After walking for another half hour, Pittsburgh plopped down on a familiar park bench. We settled down around him. We'd been here a dozen times before, but something was different that night. Pittsburgh sat there silently. Rad began playing his guitar softly- some Johnny Cash song.

Who should walk up then but Charlie: We hadn't seen since he'd left the dinner. He came right up to Jesus and gave him a fist bump. That fist bump turned out to be the first wound that Jesus would suffer that night. Out of nowhere, about seven or eight white guys with guns surrounded us. Jesus simply looked at them: *"What's going on Charlie? Why all the push? This is it – huh, Charlie? What did you tell these guys? That I was trying to start another panther gang?"* Then he paused and said to himself: *"My God, I feel so alone right now."*

At first, we thought that they were cops who were trying to pin that same old crime on Jesus. Later, however, we weren't too sure. They acted a little like cops or military commandos. None of them, however, were wearing any kind of uniforms. Their SUV looked like a squad car, but there were no D. C. police markings. Before you knew it, they grabbed Jesus and walked him to their black SUV with tinted windows was waiting. He looked back at us and shouted: *"Stay cool friends, don't worry- I'll be back."*

Evidently, Charlie had gotten a couple of G's for setting up his friend from some guy who said he worked for this group he'd never heard of before. How could Charlie have looked into Jesus eyes before selling him out? The man was a walking thunderstorm. The story I heard is that some government type-official had met Charlie at a Scottish Rite Masonic Lodge even though Charlie was Prince Hall Masonic Temple. They said something to each other about the union of a fellowship square: Water was thicker than blood. Anyway, Charlie is a dead fish already; just floating down the stream. The police report said it was a suicide; but, who knows?

Anybody could do anything if pushed far enough. Maybe that's what happened to Charlie. He was no puppet. He had his price, like we all do. His problem was that he tried to please everybody and didn't want to be different. The world is full of folks like Charlie who move in and out of the shadows; zombies without souls.

A few thuggish white GI-Joe types began to tie Pittsburgh up with plastic restraints or handcuffs. They weren't really paying much attention to us. At first, the Rock pulled out his blade and thought about cutting one of the leaders. When he saw that they were packing heat, however, he backed off.

One of their leaders turned and told us to put our hands in the air. But, since it was dark, we had no intention of staying around. We scattered: Pittsburgh, we assumed, would've done the same if he'd been in our shoes. Rock led the way. I heard the black SUV speed away. The last thing I heard was two or three quick police siren calls cutting into the heavy, cold night.

A few minutes later, we regrouped back together again. We were all sleepwalkers lost in our own thoughts. I felt sick to my stomach, filled with shame that I'd done nothing to stop those bastards when I had a chance. All I could hear was the sound of those sirens taking Pittsburgh away to God knows where. There were no angels in the sky that night – just demons inside of us filling our silent darkness.

3. A Miracle He Didn't Perform

We read, like everybody else in the newspapers the next few days, what happened next after they took him. Hatred is strong: What those racists felt about Pittsburgh was so hateful and bitter that hate wasn't a strong enough word. The SUV drove for about three hours to Lynchburg Virginia. They stopped at an abandoned barn along Thomas Road; not far from a huge church, Thomas Road Baptist.

Inside of the barn, about 60 or 70 men were waiting. They wore white robes and tall white cone shaped hats and masks covering their white faces. A burning cross was displayed in the entranceway to the barn. Some men grabbed Jesus and began to push him around their circle. Everyone was shouting.

The only one of the skinhead supremacists who wasn't wearing a hood and a white gown was distinctive for his elaborate Maori tattoos all over his arms and the fact that he was wearing a "52" Ray Lewis Baltimore Ravens jersey. He was at the center of pushing Pittsburgh around. He yelled with ferocity: *"Do you know who we are, you ugly fag N***r? Prophesy about your hell! Who hit you, boy? We got you now! How many cops have you and your boys killed? Is this how you don't answer your masters? Why don't you say something for yourself, gay-boy, tar-baby?"*

Some of the thugs around the circle held onto flaming torches. They shouted that he was a fraud. Those not holding torches began to hit Pittsburgh. The leader, with the Maori tattoos, offered Jesus some weed or booze to ease his pain and make it easier for them to beat him up: Jesus refused. Maybe seeing him stoned or drunk was their way for them to bring him down to their animal level.

They took turns spitting in his face. Some of them pulled out their Johnsons and began to piss on his face once they pushed him to the ground: *"Do you like that? You like that, don't you little girl?"*

They tried to pile on him all of their sins. At the same time, his silence made them more enraged: *"Let's take our time and kill this one, nice and good; too bad we can't kill all of them."*

Some promised to nail him to their flaming cross? Others threatened to pour gasoline all over him and set him on fire. They ripped off his clothes and then forced him to put on a FuBu basketball shirt and a Barack Obama baseball cap. They laughed that now it was just like they were getting Obama.

Pittsburgh remained silent: He had nothing to say to these fire ants swarming all over him. He was saving his strength for the future. Eventually, they became tired of their game and they tied him up. At the other end of their circle was a Virginia speed limit sign that someone had stolen for this night.

The lynching shifted into high gear. Two of them tied Pittsburgh to the street-sign. They began at him with their fists, chains, and whips. They pretended to hold a court trial: a mock judge sentenced him to death for being a fag and a ni***r: *"Here's the boy! It's up to y'all what we should do with this darkie bastard. Take him and enjoy yourself. Eat him up good boys! Make the most of him, dogs!"*

One of the Klansman hung a handmade sign around his neck that read *"King of Queers and Negroes!"* Everyone was squealing like wild hogs. Some were laughing wildly like hyenas. Their voices began to crack as they shouted: *"Yankee liberal gay dirty ni***r blood for holy pure Rebel blood! Kill him! Kill him!"* - like it was a song that they'd all learned by heart as kids. Then, more of them pulled out their knives, clubs, bats, and lead pipes.

The beating with fists, whips, and bats began. It went on until Jesus fell unconscious. Some of these goons had gone to their churches the Sunday before and had prayed to their God Almighty; they knew nothing about a God of love and mercy. The knives went in deep all over Pittsburgh. Finally, he closed his eyes. His shoulders sagged. His legs no longer carried the weight of his body. The line between heaven and earth became a dark and motionless night. He was finally able to rest.

Soon, Jesus would be home again with his mama. He'd be back with the friends who loved him. He'd be a little kid again playing in Harrisburg. He could see mama's kitchen table heavy with pies and German chocolate cake with vanilla ice cream. Pops was watching the Steelers winning a game on a TV in the background. Pittsburgh smiled faintly: He could smell mama's coffee brewing.

His face was all cut up with gashes all over. Every touch must've made his whole body go white hot in agony. He watched the thugs who were doing these things to him, but, they never really saw him. All they saw was a stereotype; an idea in their own heads that had nothing to do with him. When they tried to kill Pittsburgh; they killed the image of the God of love and mercy. Pittsburgh's body was a ripped up rag. You could still hear a faint whisper of breath. The pain must've been horrible at the end. Horrible like the pain mama felt thirty years before when he was born on that first Christmas.

4. At the Dumpster

The Klansmen uncut their ropes: They took the limp body off the speed limit sign. Amazingly, Pittsburgh still wasn't dead. They dumped him in the back of the same SUV that'd brought him. They drove him to the Garland Housing Projects, near where they'd found him. Once they had the "all clear," they dumped Jesus in an alleyway, next to a dumpster. That's where it ended for him – at a dumpster.

It was around twilight Saturday. As soon as they left a few folks came out to see what those speeding cars had dumped: Nothing good for sure. When they found Jesus they called for an ambulance. The sign *King of Queers and Negroes* was still tied around his neck. Pittsburgh was gasping weak breaths that sounded like the whispers of a child about to fall asleep. The whole history of the world was in that twisted up mess of a body. The poets and jesters are the first to die when changes come. For as long as there's been "humanity," there've been massacres, wars, and murders of the innocents.

Pittsburgh was barely breathing. His clothes were soaked in his own blood. The concrete was soaking up gallons of blood fast. A stranger told us that he tried to stop the bleeding with a towel; it was way too late. Pittsburgh was dead. It was all over.

After a little silence the folks with his body began to tell what they'd thought had happened. A minute or two later one guy began some small talk. He told whoever wanted to listen that he'd heard on the radio that the Pistons had just announced that Latrell Sprewell was finished for the rest of the season. The stranger laughed: Wasn't that a crime to kick a good man when he was down? The guy thought Spree would still make a comeback from the dead. After all of these long years, he'd probably go back to the Sixers. Why do folks chat around a corpse? I guess when you live in some places being dead and being alive aint that much different. We kept asking the folks if they'd heard Pittsburgh say anything right before he died. One boy, a kid of about sixteen, said that the last thing that he heard Jesus say was to ask for some water. Then he said something that sounded like: "*God of love and mercy, forgive all humanity-everyone. They have no idea what they were doing.*"

I don't believe what this teenager said is true. Talking about being thirsty makes sense, but, I doubt Pittsburgh was even alive by that time. Thirst is the last thing that remains; no one wants to be dry. I never remember Jesus asking for anything for himself, except for a cold glass of water from time to time, when it was hot. Asking for water made sense. The idea of forgiving folks, however, with your last breath sounds like a Hollywood try to make sense of something that made no sense. If, Jesus was even alive by then, I would've thought he would've been calling for his mama. He sure wasn't talking about forgiving some damned redneck Klansmen for smashing his head in with a baseball bat.

The official ambulance report was that Pittsburgh had died somewhere around the time that his body was dumped in the alleyway. Nobody could be exactly sure when. The folks in the project asked the ambulance-man to take the corpse. He said there was no point in taking him to the hospital. That'd just cost somebody money to get him out of the morgue. Better, he said, to find a friend, a relation, or a funeral home willing to help with the corpse. The ambulance just left.

Who knows what happened? Truth gets blown along streets littered with trash that smells like human piss and dog shit. Moldy cardboard beer cartons and ripped open garbage bags lay next to an overflowing dumpster. That's where Jesus Scott ended up. Somebody said that all of the windows in the apartment complex were shattered by a gust of wind the second Pittsburgh breathed his last breath. That was probably just a story since most of those apartments were vacant anyway.

Truth grew cold and hard like a corpse. There was blood everywhere, gallons of it, all over the place. I never knew a person could have so much blood in them.

One old man, an African named Stanley, asked some young bucks to carry the body off the street and into his apartment, a few hundred feet away. One of the on-lookers who'd once bought some crack from CJ recognized Jesus and called CJ on his cell: That's how we got the word. Meanwhile, the old African did his best to clean up a little of the blood and mud all over the corpse. CJ called a friend who worked at a funeral home. Pittsburgh was now just a weight of flesh. He was no longer a story-teller or someone who could help folks out. He was an inconvenience to folks who all just wanted to get back to sleep. He had been dropped into their laps and needed to be moved on as soon as possible.

Rad, Ced, and I got to the African's address from CJ, and knocked on his door. You could feel the dawn coming up with cold ghosts. You could hear the sighs of the dead in the sunrise. The African's apartment was like a packed slave-ship; jammed filled with ghosts. The whole city was full of phantoms. The ancestors weighed on my shoulders. The stale air around me made me feel like I was being trapped deep inside an imploding West Virginia coal mine.

Mama Shenice showed up at the door. She started to sob when she saw what they'd done to her sweet baby Jesus. Mama fell down on top of his corpse. She held it tight to herself as if it was the first time she'd ever held him like back at Magee Hospital. She was waiting for him to cry out in the way that sweet babies cry. Pittsburgh's body, in mama's arms, was finally calm; relaxed and comfortable.

Gently; after a few minutes, Rad pulled mama away from the corpse: *"I'll take care of you mama. It's gonna be all right."* This lost Catholic Irish boy in the 'hood needed mama at that moment, just as much as she needed him just then. That is the way a God of love and mercy always works things out. We folks who stay behind still need some kind of paradise until we can find something better. Mama and Rad had both been orphaned by life. They held on to each other and prayed together to Mary, the Holy Mother of God. Rad pulled out a crucifix from his pocket and gave it to mama. He prayed to her the rosary. The whole world seemed to close up on top of mama. When the undertaker finally arrived mama asked them to take her son to Pastor Lewis T. Tait Jr. at the Faith Bible Church.

5. The Funeral at Faith Bible Church

By the end of the week, nobody had been arrested for killing Pittsburgh. Further investigations were dropped. It was written off as an accident or a suicide. That took innocence or guilt right out of the equation. That was the official verdict even though when we found him we could see gashes into his skull and bruises, and even cigarette and rope burns, all over his body. His balls had been cut off. We had asked for an autopsy but none was done. The case was dropped. It was marked unsolved.

On Monday morning, an old white officer assigned to tell mama these findings, his arms filled with elaborate Maori tattoos, told her, "*Surely, your son was one of the finest Negroes that I've ever met. This young man really could've been somebody if he'd only stayed out of trouble.*" The old man's voice was hoarse. He was sucking on a throat lozenge like he'd been yelling all weekend for the 'Skins. This empty consolation made us angry for mama and sad because all of us had lost our Pittsburgh. None of us could afford a white lawyer to appeal the case: What good would that have done anyway?

At the funeral on Tuesday it seemed like everyone in town had shown up. The service was held at Faith Bible Church at 1350 Maryland Avenue North East. Heaven turned out to be, not a place of high towers and beautiful gardens, but an old grey stone building on the corner next to a gas station and a Checker's restaurant. But, there was a rightness to it because, walking up the street, I couldn't help but feel that everything that Jesus stood for could be seen on Maryland Avenue North East. This was probably the Kingdom of a God of love and mercy that I always remember him talking about.

Dr. Tait gave a beautiful service. Folks knew about the funeral because there was a note in the paper. Mostly, the article about his life mentioned that Jesus used to pick up trash with some white ladies every Saturday afternoon with a neighborhood clean-up program.

An army of mamas and sisters in the community showed up to support Mama Shenice. They were a massive school of fish swimming strong against the tide of an immensely cold, strong sea. They were experts at going to funerals. These mamas went to these funerals looking for some life for their own dead sons. Maybe mamas weeping have always been the most powerful army in world history. The sisters of D.C. were at this service simply because they had lost one of their boys at one time, and they wanted to stand beside mama and let her know that they had stood where she was now standing.

It was an ancient symphony of old, big, strong, sturdy oak-tree, tender, loving mamas as well as some willow-wispy, young, and thin, tender saplings of young sisters. They came together as sopranos, altos, and bases to make the music of their tears and to sing with weeping for their fallen sons, and for her son. They all drew from the same shared well-spring of deep pain and rock-sure understanding.

Weeping, never words, is the weapon of women in their battle against the deaths of their strong young black boys and their men taken before their time. Even when they were old men, these women who owned and cared for them still insisted that it was before their time. That was their love going out into the deep water of the next world to find a way forward.

These mamas in their black veils closed their ears to brothers around them who told them to be quiet at funerals. They'd spent enough time in their lives being silent. They remembered the pain of childbirth and the hours of nursing. They loved, only to see their gentlemen shot up in a drive-by, or knifed in prison. They knew what had happened to mama. No one could crucify the memories, frozen in time, that they held close to their breasts of their very own sweet, little, newborn, beautiful, baby boys.

These sisters brought beautiful flowers and cards to Mama Shenice. They were an army of one and a force of nature that filled up the sky like a black thundercloud that changes everything on a summer's day. For them, it mattered not in the least whether or not Jesus was some wonder-worker because all they knew was that she was mama's boy. That was enough; they were women. Every mama's boy is the one true and spotless son of god waiting in heaven to be raised again to life eternal.

We didn't even know half of the folks who brought flowers or cards. There were all kinds of folks to pay their final respects: rich and poor, young and old, black and white. Okay, truth be told, it was 90% black; but ten percent white and hispanic sure was pretty unusual around here.

Dr. Tait conducted a beautiful service. Big Sheena sang Bob Marley's *Redemption Song* which was one that Pittsburgh used to hum when walking down the street. Then the woman's chorus sang "Leaning on the Everlasting Arms." Dr. Tait read something from Malachi in the Holy Bible about justice. He preached a serious message which, thankfully, made no effort to tie anything that Pittsburgh had done in his life to the life of the Lord Jesus Christ which some folks tried to do sometimes. The preacher didn't ruin our time saying our goodbyes with a bunch of words or stupid, unimportant stuff. All of us were just thinking about Pittsburgh's smile and his way – the way he walked, and the sound of his voice.

After the service, a group of sisters pitched together to have a wonderful meal at the church hall. Everything came together. There'd been no money for a big meal but a Kenyan woman named Mrs. Chinelo, from the neighborhood clean-up program, gave an envelope to Renee at the morgue with about $10,000 in it for expenses. That was a huge amount of money: It covered everything. She wrote on the envelope one single Swahili African word that none of us could understand – *Mkombozi*.

Renee used the donation to pick out a coffin and to pay for an engraved tombstone which read: Jesus Dred Scott, One of Us- December 25, 1979 – April 4, 2009 – "Let us kill the dreamer and see what becomes of his dream."

Chapter Ten:
Resurrection and Ascension

1. *"Why are you looking among the dead for a man who's alive?"*

What I learned in the winter and spring of 2009 is that death can be a disguise. Pittsburgh, anyway, was bigger than death in the same way that he had been bigger than life.

Four days after his body was found, and a day after his funeral, three of us decided to go out to the cemetery to pay our respects. Mama Shenice, Renee, and Sheena had gone earlier to the cemetery and had left some flowers on the new grave. They had told us that the cops had stationed a guard at the cemetery to keep an eye on things. When we got there, however, the cop wasn't there. Instead, one of the cemetery maintenance guys stopped us at the gate and said strangely: *"If you're here to pay your respects to your friend, you won't find him here. He isn't here anymore."*

We went straight back to our apartment and told the others what the maintenance guy had told us. At just about the same time a Baptist pastor named Gaylon Foreman, ran into the room. He told us that he could've sworn he just saw Jesus down at Ben's Chili Bowl. He'd actually bumped into him and didn't make the connection at first since he wasn't expecting to see him there. It was all too weird.

When Ced, CJ, and I went back to the cemetery I didn't see any of the maintenance staff. We did discover that the grave of Pittsburgh had been dug up. His casket lay opened out on top of a pile of dirt; no corpse. I felt a storm of anger at whoever did this act of desecration and disrespect. CJ was screaming at the top of his lungs: *"Someone's gonna have to die whoever's messin' with us and Jesus."*

Then, sure as day, I heard the voice of Pittsburgh: *"Peace! It's me — your boy! Let's have something to eat. Calm down brothers. Dying was frightful but a God of love and mercy has changed all that. They could never win."*

There he was; standing in front of us. That's what it seemed like, at least. It seemed like Pittsburgh was right there in front of us. He looked the same as he'd looked the week before with no cuts or bruises on him. I wanted to reach over and touch him to see if he was real. It was a dream.

I closed my eyes and felt myself reaching over to this ghost. When I touched Pittsburgh he felt both as stiff as a puppet and as warm as a fire. It seemed like Jesus. He was there in flesh and blood but how can Pittsburgh be talking to us if he's a corpse?

I was dreaming. It was a magic show with a Pittsburgh hologram. We were all hallucinating what we wanted to see. Anyway, I felt like a ton of bricks was lifted off my shoulders.

Pittsburgh told us: *"I have to go now. Back to the one who sent me. Finish what I tried to start in the city. Meet me in South Philly on this day next month. Meet at 1303 Christian Street. Go and be pelicans that move all over the world feeding folks who are hurting with the strength of your blood. Be Oregon salmon swimming against the stream. Be pit bulls for old ladies who have nobody else to protect them. Wherever you go travel light - take only your bus passes and your iPods with you. Your problems aren't ending. Actually, they are just beginning. You will meet me again on the street and in the subway. subway. Go into West Philly, Trenton, Camden, and all the way to Atlantic City."* Then Jesus vanished.

The cops got involved. They reported that the gravesite had been dug up by some former Black Panthers. They called in some folks for questioning. The corpse was missing. We wondered if the Klan had desecrated the tombstone which was also gone. Maybe it was their way to try and kill him all over again. Brother Jeremy wondered if some of the Rasta's had made off with his body for one of their rituals. None of the newspapers covered this crime or, of course, to avoid wild rumors about how Pittsburgh had come back again from the dead. Jesus was already yesterday's news.

2. Life after Pittsburgh

Looking back on it all now, a few months later, I still try to figure out Pittsburgh. He was a mystery who smashed like a runaway bus into my aimless life. Since the ghost had said something about meeting in

Philly some of us went there. Nothing happened: we were chasing after dreams. Mama, Ced, Rad, Renee, Big Sheena, Manoj, CJ, and me set up in Kensington, North Philadelphia. We went like he said to Christian Street but then, after awhile, began to hang out mostly at Gray's Ferry, in Hissy Park, or around Fairmont Park. There is a great Saturday afternoon basketball program for the neighborhood kids over there. Some of us went there to help out and pass the time in Jesus' name.

Renee left our group and took a mail-clerk job at the post office of Temple University. She started a course in Afrocentric Studies at Temple. The last time I talked to her she was all excited about some books she was reading by Professor Molefi Asante, Professor Maulana Karenga, and Professor Nai'm Akbar. These brothers had a message of freedom from intellectual slavery. They were inspiring her to become a school-teacher and help little kids in the city learn how to emancipate their minds.

Rumor also has it that Renee is pregnant. Who was the father? Maybe it was Pittsburgh. If it is a boy she said she wants to name the kid Latrell Antwaan, or maybe even Jesus Latrell. Ced started working at the Divine Lorraine Hotel on Broad. Big Sheena first started working at Dot's Food for the Soul. Then she pulled a connection and got work as a shift manager at the McDonalds on the corner of Broad and Race. Manoj fell in love with a spoken-word poetry-slam guy named Righteous Watson. They were going to yoga classes together and were talking about moving up to Massachusetts to get married.

I've applied for a line job at the plastics factory in Kensington but haven't heard anything yet. We're all moving on. That's the way it always is.

Figuring things out is sometimes as hard as trying to explain music and how it touches your soul: One musician may prefer Brubeck to Mozart but that does not mean he'll not try his best to play Mozart. One thing is certain; the man Jesus was full of emotion who loved folks. It's such a shame he's no longer here to watch us all grow old and slowly decay into tired rags of preoccupied, busy old-folks errands.

Pittsburgh was both a mystery and a problem. What I mean by that is that, he's still a problem for me in the same way that the women in my life, like my complaining ex-wife or my patient African Queen, have been problems for me. They make the predictable and the smooth more unsettled by their brilliance. I love my ladies – always have - but I never understood any of them. They sure as hell – except for Africa - don't even seem to want to understand me.

One of the ways that many of us who met Pittsburgh dealt with the problems he gave us was to simply dismiss them from our minds. They transformed him into a cardboard cutout of a D. C. version of a modern-day thug-life Tupac. But, Jesus was a lot of things. He was a cappuccino drinking New York Times reading brother. He was a wanna-be musician without any formal education. He tried to be a street poet. He was a good friend, and he loved his mama, and her kitchen table growing up. Like Pastor Ron said, the brother was a voice and not just an echo: He laid down a strong, steady beat.

A lot of folks thought that Pittsburgh was a dangerous man. Following him would take all the calm and control out of their lives if they got too close to him. Probably even the Klansman who killed him were afraid of the power he had. The brother seemed peaceful even when he was down. Maybe even his enemies envied him and tried to take something from him that they wanted.

Most of all, I'm just glad that I knew Jesus Scott. Times with him were never predictable. Pittsburgh could never be controlled. Whenever I spent time with him I felt freedom growing inside me. I know that sounds corny but that's how I felt. He had a way of prospecting like a San Francisco 49er, through all of the mud that you dumped on him to find some nuggets of gold hiding deep inside.

The more I think about Pittsburgh, the more I feel that any story that I could write about him would really only be my own story cast against his canvas. Before I knew Jesus, my life was not nearly as filled with questions as it is today. Now that he's gone, Pittsburgh feels closer to me know than he ever has in my life when he was around all the time. Have you ever been on a wildly galloping horse? It's not until you get off that you realize what you were on and how wild it all was. I really wanted to write all of this down as a way for me to build my own bridge back to that time with him. But, also, and I can't quite explain this either, I feel like writing all of this has helped me somehow to get ready to see him again.

One of the things that Pittsburgh always talked about was how he relied on a God of love and mercy and God alone. That is what I'm trying to do in my own life. He would say that a God of love and mercy is watching over us. Our lives were wrapped up in a divine destiny. I never really talked much to Pittsburgh about the Lord Jesus Christ because, mostly Jesus talked about how the fire of the Holy Spirit was working everywhere in the name of Jesus.

Pittsburgh Jesus

Pittsburgh didn't pretend to have all the answers. He never acted like he had everything all figured out about life. That is one of the things I really liked about his views. Jesus seemed to have more authority when shared his view about something than anyone else I've ever known. At the same time, I never felt that he was trying to ram some idea down my throat - as if he was a salesman and the special savings were about to end within the next fifteen minutes.

Folks come and go. Jesus Scott, however, has become part of who I am. Maybe that's what he said would happen when, once while we were eating Boston Crèmes at a Dunkin Donuts he said, "*Without me you can't do anything.*"

Other folks around D.C., Baltimore, and here in Philly have been telling stories lately about meeting Jesus by surprise on the streets. It's got me lookin' up and wondering. But Pittsburgh coming back from the dead is even less likely than the Mets or Cubs ever winning a World Series again. In most of these stories that folks tell about Jesus they say that his name has been changed to Xavier or Tayla. Some of the stories say he is now going by the name of Phil Bert. Others say that he is now some kind of shoemaker from Nicaragua. The things that folks say that this person, whatever his name, is doing, however, sure remind me of Jesus Scott.

This guy who called himself Yvgeni first showed up on the CoreStates steps on the corner of Kensington and Allegheny and gave some random person six Benjamins and sixty. That sounds to me like something that Jesus would do. The same thing – and with the same amount- happened to somebody on the corner of Sixth Street and American.

One man met me on Race Street and recognized me as a friend of Pittsburgh. He told me how, one day he had been begging and a stranger came up to him and gave him some food and put him on the SEPTA near the First Union Center. When the guy thanked the stranger all that he said was that "a God of love and mercy is like a bulldog in the projects." The man said when Yvgeni paid the bus fare for him, that at that moment, he recognized that it was actually Jesus.

A homeless alcoholic on North Broad Street told about how someone had taken care of him all night keeping him warm by getting him under some blankets in a boarded up row house off of Lehigh Street and in the morning took the man to the Gallery to buy some new clothes. The brother was sure it was Jesus but the guy said that his name was Phil Bert. That also sounds like Pittsburgh. Someone else said they saw him at Xando's and the Last Drop up in the upper class neighborhoods of Walnut and Chestnut driving off in a SAAB convertible. Somebody else said they thought they saw him baptizing some kids in a park fountain up in Northeast Philly.

The last story like this that I heard folks tell was at an April 4 Martin Luther King Memorial service where somebody swears that Pittsburgh showed up in the back pew and stayed throughout the service. It was the spitting image but the visitor's card that the guy filled out said that his name was "Miguel." Maybe he's still moving around Kensington, Philly, or has moved on to sidewalks, alleyways, and street corners somewhere else, in some other state, or maybe in some other country. I remember he told me once that he always wanted to hit the road as a traveler with no clock to punch or no electricity bills to pay.

Maybe Jesus went down to Sao Paulo in Brazil. He once fell in love with a girl from Jardim Icarai. She had given him a standing invitation to meet her parents and have a glass of suco maracuja with her whenever he was in town. It was the only time I ever heard him talk about falling in love, although the girl did sound like she was half crazy and half filled with fear.

Maybe it was vulnerability that Pittsburgh most admired in his friends. Some folks want to try to be a savior for someone and if they can't change the whole world they just settle down with some lady - and her crazy cats - and try to make a difference there. Pittsburgh used to talk about how he loved Brazilian soccer, especially a team dressed in black named "Corinthians." He'd said he always wanted to go to Brazil if he ever got the chance and watch them play. Maybe now he has taken that chance.

This may sound a little strange but I still talk to him. It makes me feel better. I'm not one to look back, but everything seems turned upside down now. Nothing seems to have ended and everything seems to be goin on like normal. If Jesus is up in some big mansion in heaven like some people say he must be by now, I hope he has good box seats for the Knicks games or Phils games if he can see them from up there. He sure loved himself some ball.

As I write all of this down it is still fresh in my mind. I'm working on a laptop that my grandma had given to me. I just bought a Philadelphia Inquirer and a cup of coffee. The paper says the Dali Lama and a delegation of Tibetan Monks are coming to town for a rally. If I were on the lookout for a sighting of Jesus then that would be, I think, a good place to go.

There is an interesting article today in the paper about the survivors of the Armenian Genocide. It talks about how even the United States government refuses to recognize the murder of over a million of these

Christian people so as not to offend the Turks. For some folks, I guess, the truth is not the truth. There is another article about the MOVE brothers, all named Africa, who were shot to hell here in the 80s by Frank Rizzo or one of those other clowns – the folks who locked up Mumia for that cop, Daniel Fitz, and who all eat their cheese-steaks at Geno's: Dead fish just go with the flow. Thinking about it now, I wish Jesus could've tried one of Pat's cheese-steaks straight up. Pat's a good man. But, then again, he might actually be sitting at Pat's right now. Maybe I should go and see? It feels nice to think like this. Life never seems long enough for the important things like Pat's, or strong, fresh coffee, or good seats behind home plate at a ball game, does it?

This place where I am writing this now has Wi-Fi connection and the owners let me sit here as long as I want. They just leave me alone whenever things are slow; which is most of the time. Anyway, I buy my share – and keep just enough in my cup to make me look like I've got a right to be using up a table. The only bad thing about this place is the radio station in the background plays music that I wouldn't wish on my worst enemy. It is that white-people-being-angry heavy-metal acid-music stuff. Do you know the stuff I'm talking about? No real beat but heavy on crappy, fake, deep, deepness.

That's about it for me. I'm at this Sushi Bar on the corner of Fifth and Division here in Philly. Its lunchtime and the folks out on the street are surging by as if nothing that I've written about ever actually happened. As long as there are folks on the move- too busy for a coffee or to stop and listen to a story - then we'll still need to have story-tellers, musicians, clowns, and poets who'll go to the streets.

I need to tell you one last thing before I let you go on your way: Yesterday, the weirdest thing happened to me. Near Needle Park a woman ran up to me frantically. She was carrying her baby girl. She said: *"Can you help me mister?! Please! Oh my God! My girl just stepped on a needle What if...."*

I have no idea where it came from, but a thought came into my mind. What would Pittsburgh do in this same situation? I looked at the lady. I had this unexplainable confidence that bordered on foolishness. Something came out of my mouth from out of nowhere: *"Sister. Just believe. Your baby'll be fine. The user of this needle didn't have AIDS. Your kid won't have even as much as an ear infection."*

"Are you sure? Thank you! And thank God Almighty, mister Mexican man."

"No, thank a God of love and Mercy!"

I guess the basic thing about his life meeting mine is that the music is still playing. I still remember the tune and still want to dance. We all have to find our own way out of the maze but part of the satisfaction is the friends we meet along the way. Life is both random and comfortable when you live it day to day and in the moment. We adjust: All the stuff we faced yesterday prepares us for all the stuff we'll face tomorrow.

Around every street corner, and in every hallway, I'm still looking for Pittsburgh. I'm still waiting to bump into him, see his smile, feel his embrace, and hear his voice. I miss him. I miss his compassionate curiosity. I miss how he wasn't afraid to question or take a risk without worrying about money or what other people would think. I miss how when he met an addict he would re-label, and re-value them as angels. I miss how he would re-attribute a social problem to be a cry from the heart. He was a creative brother with a free and generous soul. Nothing you gave to Pittsburgh, not even a minute of your time or an ounce of your energy, was ever lost.

It's confusing: But, if I could do it all over again, I'd still follow him. Hope is stamped inside of all that I am and all that I want to be. Pittsburgh is in my heart and in my family of memories now. If I close my eyes right now, I tell you, I can still hear his laughter and the soft swerves of his voice. He still lives.

Postscript: Two Friends

The Reverend Dred "Perky" Scott was born on June 19, 1948 in Harrisburg, Pennsylvania. He received a Bachelor's Degree from the University of Minnesota, the Indiana University of Pennsylvania, and both a Masters and a Juris Doctorate Degree from the University Of Pittsburgh School Of Law. He is presently the Pastor of St. Matthew UMC in Dundalk, Maryland where he has been pastoring for thirteen years. Before that Dr. Scott served as Senior Pastor of the Abba African Methodist Episcopal Zion Church in Harrisburg, PA.

Dr. Scott has released a number of musical recordings including *Extremity, Playing our Dues,* and *Live at the Whitaker Center- Nine* from his work as a member of the Jazz in the Sanctuary Ensemble. Dr. Scott travels throughout the country speaking and ministering in music. He is married to the former Katherine Marshall and they are the parents of two adult daughters, Khaleedah Jones and Wakeelah Falls and three grandchildren Lyndale, Troy and Deshawn.

Dr. A. Christian van Gorder was born in Pittsburgh on April 30, 1960. He received a Bachelor's Degree from Oral Roberts University, Master's from Asbury Theological Seminary and a Doctorate of Philosophy from the Queen's University of Belfast, Ireland. He is Associate Professor of World Religions at Baylor University in Waco, Texas, where he has been teaching for the last seven years. Before that, Dr. van Gorder taught at Messiah College in Grantham, Pennsylvania and at the Yunnan University in Kunming, China. In 2010-2011, Dr. van Gorder serves as a visiting lecturer in the Department of Religious Studies at the University of South Florida where Dr. Mozella Mitchell resides as chair. Dr. van Gorder is the author of *Three Fifth's Theology* (2004) and (2011) *Red, White, Black and*

Blue: Racism in Obama's America with Dr. Lewis T. Tait, Jr.; *No God but God; Christians in Persia;* and *Muslim-Christian Relations in Central Asia*. He is married to Vivian Ndudi Ezeife and has six children: Patrick Xavier, Brendan Daniel, Keegan Evangeline, Sean Michael, Tatijana Erika, and Gretchen Michele.

The mutual friendship that Dr. Scott and I share began in Harrisburg in 2000 and has remained a source of brotherly nurture, encouragement, and artistic, creative inspiration through good times and bad during those years. I love the good doctor for so many reasons. He is easily one of the most creative and godly people that I have ever had the privilege of knowing in my life. The brother is a devout man of faith who has never allowed judgmentalism to take root in his life. He has walked a very different journey than have I but, in our friendship and in our shared teaching experiences, he has shared much of his heart with me. Knowing Dr. Scott has never been boring. Thank you for everything, dear friend.

Most of all, the two of us share in common a love for Jesus, his people, the community of the beloved, and each other. I've written this book from the heart of our friendship and in the spirit of a shared conviction that our God of love and mercy is at work through the creativity of the Holy Spirit in our world today. Through life, we can both attest with a brother of old: "*There is none like the Galilean.*"

CPSIA information can be obtained at www.ICGtesting.com
Printed in the USA
244226LV00002B/157/P